PRAISE FOR ROOTWORK

"*Rootwork* is one part magical realism, one part coming of age story, one part examination of American identity, and all parts pure magic. It's unique and spellbinding, and I loved it."

—Lisa Morton, six-time winner of the Bram Stoker Award

"With *Rootwork*, Tracy Cross introduces herself to readers as a gifted storyteller of the highest order. This is a richly folkloric tale of traditions passed down, or community and family, and the lasting links forged through the shared experiences of sisters and the impenetrable bonds that anchor them to their histories and each other. At the heart of *Rootwork* is its plucky, free-spirited heroine, Pee Wee Conway, who is certain to beguile readers of all ages."

—Vince A. Liaguno, Bram Stoker Award-winning editor of *Unspeakable Horror: From the Shadows of the Closet and Other Tales: An Inclusive Anthology*

"*Rootwork* fearlessly brings folk horror to the Deep South. Tracy Cross paints a dark portrait of Black family life, with all the wisdom of our ancestors—their accomplishments, their sorrows, their unresolved hope and rage—and in doing so delivers uniquely American horror without pulling any punches. If you're a fan of historical fiction and tales of the supernatural, this book will resonate with you long after you're done reading it."

—John Edward Lawson, author of *Bibliophobia*

"Rootwork transported me to another world, on I was unfamiliar with but thoroughly enjoyed. Blending history, hoodoo, and horror elements, Tracy Cross delivers a compelling narrative with characters I sincerely hope to meet again. I really did feel like I was right there alongside Pee Wee and Aunt Teddy."

—Janine Pipe, Splatterpunk Award-nominated author of *Sausages: The Make of Dog Soldiers*

"The power and promise of fiction is the ability to take you places you can't go and do things you'll never do with people you'll never meet. Rootwork delivers on that promise with an engrossing coming-of-age tale set amid the voodoo and hoodoo of backcountry Louisiana in 1889. Tracy Cross works magic with the characters and setting of her debut novel. You will love this book and the people in it."

—F. Paul Wilson, author of *The Keep*

"*Rootwork* is a love letter to Black American spirituality, history, and resilience. Much like the work of Zora Neale Hurston, Tracy Cross's debut novel demystifies and uplifts the medicinal and magical practices of rootwork in Black communities while never straying from its true mission: to tell you a story about a family that loves, fights, and heals. In this time of upheaval and uncertainty, *Rootwork* is the kind of novel you want to curl up with at the end of the day. It is a story that reminds us of the courage and love we hold in our hearts."

—Wi-Moto Nyoka, Head Spooky Chick at Black Women Are Scary podcast, and Dusky Projects

ROOTWORK

Rootwork © 2022 Tracy Cross

Edited by Marissa van Uden
Book Design and Layout by Rob Carroll
Cover Art by Ryan Mills
Cover Design by Rob Carroll

ISBN 978-1-958598-01-6 (paperback)
ISBN 978-1-958598-14-6 (ebook)

darkhartbooks.com

ROOTWORK

CONJURE SERIES, BOOK ONE

TRACY CROSS

*This book is dedicated to my Grandma and Grandpa Cross,
Grandma Katie Mae, Grandpa Eddie Lovelace, Great Aunts
Betty and Lois, and of course, my Mom and Dad.*

SUMMERTIME
1889

Pee Wee, the youngest and boldest of her sibling explorers, took off running through the woods to beat her sisters home. The sun whispered through the trees, shining on her red-brown skin. Her jet-black pigtails bobbed as she ran fast, chin high, sweeping past the willow trees and feeling the soft Spanish moss beneath her shoes, stray twig bushes swatting her legs, all while carefully skipping or jumping every mud puddle in the humid parish backwaters, knowing she didn't want to splash-up her good white knee socks, even if one sock did hang around her ankle, for this was not just a day leading into summer break. It was something much more special.

The last day of school was always exciting for Pee Wee, Betty, and Ann Conway, mostly because it meant they were free to roam all the parts of the parish they did not know, especially its dark side.

Pa was coming home with the promise of sweets, and she couldn't wait to taste them.

"Slow down! Ain't no fire!" Ann's shrill voice nipped at her heels only making her fly faster.

"No, no, I can't wait to see Pa. I been waiting to see him all spring. Wrote me a letter sayin' he bringin' some car'mels! And I been *extra* good. Got me all good marks on my card. He promised them to me!"

"Hattie, you's a liar! You made them marks on that card y'self. Ma ain't stupid. She gonna beat yo ass when she find out."

Pee Wee, ever on the move, slowed and sassed Ann. "Don't call me *Hattie*. Name's Pee Wee, girl. And I'm a tell her you been cussin' and kissin' them mixed boys down in the bayou."

"You gonna do no such thing, or I'm a call you a liar!"

Pee Wee doubled down and increased distance. "Everybody know, Ann! Whatcha gonna do when you gets pregnant? With a lil mixed baby? Shoot, some white folk gonna snatch him up, talkin' bout 'Look at how purty his skin is. This here *ours* now. Them ol' nappy heads in that parish sure can make good lookin' car'mel babies.'"

Betty, tawny-skinned enough to almost pass for white, her springtime hair clipped short, came not far off Ann's flank, slowed to a stop, and doubled over, wiping at her freckled face, her voice sober. "Y'all, that ain't funny, Hattie Mae."

Pee Wee slowed and trotted backward. "Ann call me a liar. Do I lie?"

"Now you just bein' mean. 'Sides, who you sayin' nappy? You the nappy head. Look here! Mama press a comb to it this morn, now it look nappier than that time you fell in that mud patch."

"I may haves that nappy hair, Bettina Jean, but I's gonna see Daddy faster than you!"

Ann laughed as she caught up steady, one mocha-colored hand grabbing at Pee Wee's white blouse, her skin reddish. The last sunburn she had laid her up and made her bedridden for two days, and she was getting ruddy.

"When I catch you, Pee Wee, I'm a kick your ass for talkin' too much!"

Pee Wee shoved her sister off, spun, and kept running. "And I'm a tell mama you's cussin'!"

Ann ran up beside Pee Wee. "And there you go! Talkin' too much, again!"

Betty smiled as she zipped by them both. "No school, Daddy home. Life ain't get no better, sisters!"

The trio ran along the path, each teasing at the other until they arrived breathless at their cabin, whose stilts stood on the firm ground of a clearing surrounded by tall wild oaks. The stilts were high enough to keep the house from flooding when the heavy rains fell in the summer. One year, the water flooded the cabin, and Ma lost everything, including her precious quilts from her mother. She wagged a finger at Pa and told him to make sure this never happened again. He measured the highest water mark and built the stilts to sit higher because even Pa was afraid of Ma from time to time. Several other homes, similar in size, clustered in a half circle, while off to the left leaned the weeping willows that led to the nearby fishing hole. Beyond all that: a field of wild cotton they each could pick and harvest unto themselves, because they were blessed enough to own the land.

Pee Wee, Ann, and Betty all considered their home as a comforting and restful place, and each of them had a space slightly bigger than most for themselves. There were two bedrooms, an attic (which the girls shared, divided by clotheslines and makeshift curtains that Betty made), a huge living room, and a wide front porch, which, like its humble neighbors, had a few short steps up to the front door. Their daddy worked both construction and along the railroad and was able to add such extras himself, if only so he and Ma had a place to sit out and smoke their pipes. He even painted the window borders haint blue, just to keep the bad spirits away, and when he finished, neighbors fought to pay him for the rest of the slather. Daddy refused, instead sending them to a man in town to help his business. That man, grateful for the customers, told Daddy that if he ever needed anything, all he'd have to do was holler.

The land around them was so dirt-worn that if someone wanted to hold a meeting, everyone would just drag a chair or something to sit on and there'd be speaking, usually beneath a huge tree at the heart of the cabin circle. Sometimes there'd be a huge party in the same place just to end the summer, where the men dragged up logs to build a circle-fire with a blaze big enough to roast covered pots of boiling crawfish, catfish soup, beans, and rice all at once. Some members of the Natchez Tribe and their wives shared their spices, added them to the stews, and the aroma of the cooking made the whole town smell so delicious you wished you could eat the air. Even the Cajuns would come looking for a morsel, knowing their cooking was too hot to taste for anyone there, except maybe Pa and Pee Wee, who ate it all up without a blink.

When the sisters stopped at the front door to wipe the mud from their shoes, the air was scented with baking bread. Their mother swept at the porch, the broom's whisk blending that aroma with the new honeysuckle that curled and crept along the ground outside the cabin like sleeping snakes. The aroma spelled not only the treat of fresh baking but also of new butter for the girls, who loved coming home to both and would beg to see it fresh-churned. They would stuff themselves so full before dinner that their appetites would be joyously spoiled, and this happened often enough that Ma, the master baker, couldn't even get mad anymore.

Ma nodded as she swept. "How was school today?"

The girls answered in unison: "Fine, ma'am."

Then Pee Wee came forward, fidgeting. "I got some good marks on my card!" she said, handing her mother the paper.

Mama held the paper a distance from her eyes. "Mm-hmm," she purred. Then she waved it in the air before pressing it to her ample bosom. "Sure you ain't write these in yourself? Look like some scribbles I done seen before."

Pee Wee feigned sincerity, rising onto her toes. "Promise! Pa come home?"

"I dunno. Depends on your sisters' grades." Ma held out her sand-colored hand, itself as covered with freckles as Betty's face. "Bettina, Patricia Ann…y'all's marks?"

Each came to her, papers out, and she eyed them with a mix of suspicion and humor. After a few moments, she laughed, loud and hearty. "Pa, c'mon out! Your girls is smart *and* home!"

A comforting footfall bumped off the wood as Robert Conway, a huge, strapping man, skin shining and clean as new molasses, stepped onto the newly swept porch, his short hair cascading in waves across his head. He held a raggedy towel up to his face and wiped it dry.

He held his arms out to them. "There's my girls!"

Pee Wee laughed. "Good thing you's a big man, Pa. Else you can't catch us all!"

"I missed y'all bunches! And before you even ask, yes, Pee Wee, I gotcha car'mels." The girls stood around him while he dug deep into his pockets. "I think I gots one for each one of y'all. And maybe a few extras."

Betty took the entire handful and ran into the cabin. Pee Wee shuffled after her, almost bumping into her.

Ann remained on the porch. She clasped her hands behind her back and leaned back on her heels.

"Patricia Ann, did ya wanna talk 'bout somethin'?" Pa pulled out a pipe, sat in a chair, and lit it.

Ma set the broom against the door, pulled out her own pipe, and lit it as she sat next to him.

"Not really. I mean, I just was wonderin' 'bout if we can visit your sister over the break. That one that Ma don't like. 'Haps I can earn some money doin' work around her place."

Ma and Pa sucked on their pipes for a long time in silence. Ma opened her mouth, but Pa placed a hand on hers and patted it.

"Lemme think 'bout it. I just got home, y'know," he said. "But I don't see no harm in y'all earnin' a lil money…"

Ma's face turned bright red. She spoke through gritted teeth: "Workin' for some conjure woman—What's Ann goin' to do, Robert? Boil cats and skin frogs? Y'know your sister don't make much a nothin'. People gots to leave her offerings cuz she ain't s'posed to ask for money!"

Pa leaned back in his chair and smiled. "Ain't nothin' wrong with the girls spendin' time sweepin' and runnin' errands once in a while. 'Sides, my sis always been like that. She wasn't never one to ask for much. It's also the code: gotta give to get, y'know?"

Ma blew some smoke out the side of her mouth. "Says you. And how much you bring back this here time, Mister Traveler?"

"Sorry, Ma and Pa. I'm a do my chores now, if'n that's okay." Ann eased inside before they started arguing about money. Pa could spend it faster than he got it. Ma said Pa holding on to money was like trying to grip a wet eel.

Pee Wee, after running to get the empty clothes basket and pull the clothes off the line outside, struggled to get in through the tiny hallway. Betty blocked her and the doorway, holding a cleaver in her hand ready to go get dinner: a chicken from a few houses over.

"You need to move over so I can get dinner," Betty said.

"You need to move over lest you want your stank clothes. I will show everybody your bloomers." Pee Wee said.

Betty shot Pee Wee a glare before easing past her and out the door.

"Y'all takin' somethin' from the garden for that chicken?" Ann asked.

"Ma already took care," Betty said. "I's just takin' my cleaver to knock out them boys that block my way. You know, like Gene."

"The one with the Indian ma?" Ann asked. "He sure is pretty, for a boy. You should think 'bout him 'cause he like you an awful lot. And they gots money. Least that's what I heard. And Ma asked me to get more stuff from the garden, on account of Pa bein' extra hungry."

"What you mean, 'that's what you heard'?" Betty set the cleaver down on a stool by the back door and put one hand on her hip.

"Well, his mee-maw is half white. I seen her in town, talkin' to the sheriff. Sheriff was smilin' and what not. She look real white, it's why he like talkin' to her."

"We can pass. Well, maybe not you. Pee Wee can't, unless Ma press your hair and you don't sweat it out before you get to town." Betty laughed, picked up the cleaver again, and stepped out the door. "You comin'? Gotta get them chores done, and that laundry ain't gonna fold itself."

Pee Wee picked up the basket and walked like she was a rich woman, her nose high in the air. "Thanks, kind lady, for holdin' that door open. I's appreciate it."

"You sure is stupid! But you make me laugh with your stupid self."

Betty and Pee Wee broke up laughing.

Pee Wee asked, "If'n you help me with the foldin', can I walk with ya to get that chicken?"

"Sure, why not?"

"Y'all eat all them candies?" Ann yelled from the step. She stood in the doorway, tying her apron around her waist. "I mean, they is the only real sweets we get once in a while."

Pee Wee put her hands on her hips. "We left yours on your bed. Go on!"

"She always act like she the oldest of us," Betty mumbled, "makin' plans and everything. She ain't the boss of me."

"All of fourteen and you so tough." Pee Wee elbowed Betty.

"Better than to be ten and scramblin' behind everybody sniffin' at they buts!" Betty nudged her back.

Betty ran and grabbed one end of the sheet off the clothesline, and Pee Wee held the other. The way they folded the sheet was like a dance: in then out, down and up.

"Hey, y'all, listen," Ann said. "I got an idea. How 'bout we stop by Pa's sis's house on the way to get that chicken?"

Betty and Pee Wee looked at each other.

"You done lost your mind!" Pee Wee took the sheet from Betty and dropped it in the basket. "That's clear on the other side of the pond!"

"I asked if I could work over there this summer." Ann raised her chin. "And Pa said yes."

"Bull!" Pee Wee and Betty said in unison.

"He did, and I'm goin'. Probably end of next week." Ann nodded to emphasize it.

"Ain't no way," Betty said. "'Sides, Ma hates Auntie. Don't you remember when she brought them bones over here and a bucket a pee? Talkin' 'bout how we needed protection. When Ma saw 'em under the porch, she like to had a stroke! Can't say it didn't work, though. For one week, everything was okay."

"Bones and pee!" Pee Wee made a face. "Eww!"

"You see them houses painted that 'haint blue'?" Betty asked. "She gave us that paint too."

"I heard the sheriff and them white boys in town like her a lot," Ann said. "Guess it's because of what she can do."

"Where you hear this?" Betty grabbed some pants off the clothesline, folded them, and dropped them into the basket.

"Don't matter. It's what I heard."

Pee Wee glared at Ann. "Look, I gotta get this done, or else Ma is gonna beat my ass. And I wanna go with Betty to get the chicken."

ANN

"**P**atricia Ann!" Ma called. "Get some more vegetables since your Pa is here. He like to eat everything in sight. Pee Wee and Betty went to get the chicken."

"Ma, I just wanted to take a walk!" Ann said.

"Then walk over to the garden and get the vegetables!"

Ann kicked at the dirt and headed towards the garden.

Even though she had to head to the garden, she liked walking alone. It was nice to be surrounded by quiet instead of competing with Pee Wee and Betty to see who could talk the most or the loudest. Ann liked the silence because she spent a lot of time in her thoughts. Her thoughts were of becoming someone big and powerful. Somebody to command respect when those white boys came to town looking for something.

Ann saw a little dark-skinned boy that lived near Cousin Skeet running towards her. She didn't know his real name but around the village he was called "Bump." He jumped around like a June bug and talked twice as fast as the other kids.

"Ann! Ann! Where ya goin'? Can I come?" He doubled over next to her and caught his breath.

"So much for bein' alone in my thoughts," Ann said.

He jumped onto the logs that lined the path to the community garden, flipping over a few of them. That made her laugh. He was a clumsy boy, all long limbs like a colt.

"Bump, whatcha doin' out here alone? Where Skeet?"

The boy jumped in the air and spread his arms out, balancing on a log. "I dunno. I saw ya walkin' and I wanted to come see where you was goin'."

"I'm gonna mind my business." Ann made a gesture like she was going to push him off.

"You goin' to the garden? Can I help ya carry stuff back? I got me a basket there for helpin.'"

Although she wouldn't have the time alone in her head she wanted, she laughed and motioned for him to come along with her.

The garden was a bit away from where they lived, over a wide wooden bridge that had seen better days. Hay was stacked at the beginning and along the bridge, and a combination of hay and dirt covered the bridge as Ann kicked her way across it. The land on this side of the river was more fertile, she was told. Everything grew like crazy, and all the animals liked it as well. This was where they kept the horses and cows. An Indian named Lone Wolf lived over here and kept an eye on things. The Cajuns were always close by, ready for anything to happen.

Bump kept talking nonstop: "…and I call this the straw bridge, cuz they put straw on the part we walkin' on…"

Ma gotta get up and go to work every day. The way she talk about Pa's sister makes me think I should try and do something else. Not workin' for somebody, but make everybody come to me. She don't never say that 'the swamp rat' gotta go to the city. She say how everybody come to her. Aunt Teddy ain't got a man; she just got herself. Least that's what Ma say.

I wonder if Aunt Teddy went to school? Maybe she been on her own for a long time. Mostly everybody here got a man or a baby nipping behind them. I don't never hear her say nothin' like that about Aunt Teddy. Aunt Teddy livin' free and go where she want. She live by her own rules and makin'. I would love to live alone in the bayou, catchin' fish, doin' whatever and maybe…maybe I find a good man to have around to fix things. Make himself useful in ways men are useful. Not naggin' me 'bout no supper or what I do all day.

Maybe, just maybe, if I train with Aunt Teddy, I can get a job in the city. I know I can make a lot of money pretending to know more than those wannabe voodoo white women downtown. If them white womens can pretend to know something and make money, imagine what they would do with a black girl that knew what she was doing. Nothing but respect for me, and all them old white ladies can go back to sippin' tea...

"Ann! We almost there! I hope I can catch a grasshopper. I wanna catch some good fish—not catfish—for dinner."

"Yeah, Bump. Where do you go to catch fish?" She unlatched the gate and walked down the rows, looking at all the vegetables: bright yellow squash almost pulling themselves free from the vine, collard greens as big as elephant ears, and okra sweeping up toward the sky—the hard pods followed the direction of the sun and grew straight up. She plucked a few, and then headed over to the lettuces and cucumbers in the far corner. She pulled out a huge knife and started cutting away.

"You want me to pull some potatoes? I can do that because I know where they at."

"Pull the potatoes, Bump." Ann laughed to herself. *If kids are this annoying, I ain't havin' none. Gonna find me a rich man and go round the world, tellin' fortunes and doing rootwork. I'm gonna be so rich that nobody will ever call me out my name again.*

'Sides, in a year, Betty's gonna be gone. They want me to go to finishing school with her but never asked me what I wanted to do. I wanna do rootwork. I wanna be like Aunt Teddy.

"This enough?" Bump held up several carrots.

"I thought you was pullin' potatoes." Ann stood and put her hand on her lower back.

"Oh!" He looked at the carrots. "I can take 'em home and ask Skeet to make me a stew or somethin'. All this is hard work." He laughed, dropped the carrots in his basket and went to dig for potatoes. "Only, thems my carrots. Don't take 'em, okay?"

"Bump, how old are you?"

"Old enough for you." Bump looked up at her, a smudge of dirt on his nose.

"You thought about whatcha want do in your life? Like leave this place and go somewhere else?"

Bump tilted his head and stared. "Well, all I know is this place. The world is so big. And I'm so small. But when I grow up taller"—he motioned with his hand up high—"I'm gonna get me a job and make so much money. World best watch out for me." His voice trailed off.

Not me. I'm gonna leave this town and take as much knowledge with me that I can. I can read, write, and clean, but I'm not gonna be like Ma, waitin' for Pa to bring money home. I'm a have my own money and my own place to live. I'll even get Betty her own horse.

Bump dropped the potatoes in the basket, startling her. "Sorry, Ann! I ain't know you was thinkin'. You look like you wanted to say somethin'."

"I was gonna say that I gotta get home to make dinner. I got some other plans to start makin'." Ann picked up the full basket and put it on her hip. "Lock the gate behind me. And don't forget your carrots. We sure don't eat 'em"

Bump's back was to her. She looked at his dirty bare feet, his cut-off pants that hung on his skinny frame, his old blue T-shirt with holes in it. She smiled and pulled the carrots out the basket. "Eat these and you'll get big and strong."

"I'm already strong!"

"Not as strong as me, cuz I'm gonna leave this place," Ann mumbled, and they began walking back to the cabins.

"You say somethin', Ann?" Bump called.

"Nothin' you'd understand." Ann said.

Bump scratched his head before yelling, "Ann! Ann! Don't forget to bring my basket back!"

THE JOURNEY

The early-morning sunlight filtered through the sheer curtains of the attic, lighting up the speckles of dust drifting in the air. Ma waved the dust out of her way as she walked into the room. Each girl slept in her own bed, which served as a look into each of their personalities. Pee Wee's wooden bed frame was covered with heavy black scribblings and copies of symbols she saw outside on some of the other cabins. Ann's had roses painted on the headboard, herbs on the foot of her bed, and vines crawling up the outside of the wooden frame. Betty slept on an extravagant bed with a mosquito net that the sisters would crawl under once in a while. When they huddled together, Betty would always remind them that she made it herself and that they should always thank her. She also made pillows all the time from the softest fabric she could find.

"I know, since Pa come home and we been eatin' good, ain't no reason to get lazy," Ma said as she woke them all up. "Now, since y'all wanna learn 'bout rootwork, here's the plan. Y'all gets to go see your pa's sister for the whole day. Come back and tells me whatcha learned. And maybe go back out there tomorrow."

"Ma!" Pee Wee yelled, sitting up in the bed. "I ain't wanna go! That was all Ann!"

"Don't make no difference. Pa thought it'd be a good idea for y'all to go together. You know where that swamp rat live, don't ya?" Ma put her hands on her hips. "Down near where the creek run off to the right. She live near the levee. I done packed some hoecakes and stew. Should last ya two meals, if'n y'all don't get greedy. Now, get up, get dressed, and get downstairs!"

"What 'bout for later, Ma? You pack us some food for later?"

"That swamp rat Teddy can feed ya. I ain't got no time. And I'll tell you what, when y'all come back, tell me if ya wants to work for her all summer, okay?"

Ma walked down the stairs from the attic. She stopped at the bottom and yelled up, "An layin' in bed cryin' about it ain't goin' to do ya no good. So, come on downstairs!"

The girls shuffled around, pulling themselves together slowly, but they paused all movement when they heard Pa's voice rising up from downstairs: "Ma, forgot to tell ya. Guess who I ran into the other day?"

"Dunno," Ma replied.

"Sheriff come askin' me for a donation for somethin' in town. I told him he should be payin' for all these babies he got everywhere. Man got a thing for our women."

"What he say?" Ma's voice had moved around.

"What they talkin' 'bout?" Ann whispered.

Betty scooted to the top of the stairs and made a shush motion with her finger to her lips. "I dunno. Maybe Pa done did somethin' again."

"He say, 'Well, you pay for the babies, and I'll keep makin' 'em.' He don't even care how half these little back squats ain't nothin' but his lil mixed kids with poor mothers. Young girls that ain't finished school. Got no kinda life but waitin' for that man to come and spill all up in 'em and hope he give 'em some money or somethin'."

"I don't like that man," Ma said. "If he ain't makin' babies, he snatchin' up our girls to sell off to his wife and her kin folk. Maybe he keep 'em to work in his house. You know, Buck used to work for him, and he said he had all kinds a kids everywhere. Where he find these lil young girls?"

Pa said, in a low voice, "These girls are *our* girls. You know that Ma. He just come and take his pick of 'em."

Ma made a sound, like she agreed.

"Most of these women don't want nothin' to do with him. He best not come round here. I'd shoot him first and ask questions later, ya know."

Betty and Ann looked at each other, wide-eyed. Pee Wee covered her mouth and gulped.

"What's that mean?" she asked.

"Nothin' good." Betty whispered.

"If'n you can find the shotgun. Then, the bullets."

"Maybe you underestimate me, woman. Maybe, just maybe, I got my own lil piece a somethin' I keep close by."

"Lord, Pa, we don't need no more problems in this house." Ma walked away from him and pulled something from the stove. "Almost made me burn this cornbread."

"You know, Ma. I been thinkin' that we should find somewhere else to live. I mean, up North, I done seen a black man get treated with respect. White men treatin' us like equal, workin' side by side on the tracks or at the factories. You know, feels like we always waitin' for a flood to drive us out or somethin'. I tell ya', the North is like a whole new world."

"Well, Pa, we don't live up North."

"I keep tellin' ya, we should move up there. Take the girls, get 'em a fine education."

"Like your sister?" Ma's voice cut across the room.

"Yeah, matter of fact, just like my sister."

"They can come back here and be swamp rats just like her."

"Aw, Ma, maybe we got us another Nat Turner in one of them girls."

The sound of Ma's laugh filled the room. "Nat Turner was too smart for his own good. Where he now? Dead, that's what. You wanna kill our girls?"

"Ma, is much more to it than that, you know." Pa sighed. "I mean, when I was on the railroad in Ohio, I heard a black woman done graduated college. School was called 'Ober-lain' or somethin' like that. Imagine us havin' three girls like that. Everybody round here would respect us. Them rich womens from the city would probably come ask them for advice. And maybe they even buy a nice place near where that LaLaurie place was so we can look down our noses at white folk."

"You sure is a big dreamer and a knucklehead, Pa."

"You don't think our girls is smart enough?"

Pee Wee pointed at Betty and whispered, "He talkin' bout you, cuz I knows I'm smart."

"Smart enough to draw dumb stuff all over your bed," Betty snapped.

"But I sleep better at night and not moanin' 'bout some boy." Pee Wee wrapped her arms around herself and made kissing sounds.

Ann reached out and covered their mouths. "Y'all shut up! I can't hear nothin'!"

"…smart as a whip." Ma's voice rose up the stairs. "They can choose to do what they want and I hope they leave this place!"

Their voices seemed to move closer. Perhaps Pa was slipping behind Ma the way he did, wrapping his hands around her waist. "What's with all the fussin' ?"

"Nothin' Pa, is just hard because I want them girls to decide they own destiny. We made ours and let them make theirs. Besides, I told them they could go see your sister for a day or so." Ma's voice sounded stressed. "Is that all right with you?"

"Why not let them girls stay for a few days? We could get us some time together." Pa crooned, letting the baritone in his voice smooth over any problems she may have had.

"This must of been like when they was courtin'," Betty whispered, "on account of how Pa sound like he tryin' to get her to do somethin' she don't wanna."

"Is that how Gene sound, Betty?" Ann asked.

Betty shot her a glare, and Ann shrugged.

The three girls finished dressing and crept down the stairs. Sunlight flooded through the windows and streamed across the floor, slinking its way over the threadbare red carpet. They watched their massive father envelop their mother, who giggled and covered her face. She laughed while he whispered stuff in her ear. She wrapped her arms around his and giggled even more—until she realized the girls were standing there, watching.

"Uh, why don't ya stay with your pa's sister for a few days. Give me and Pa some time to uh…" Ma stumbled as she fixed her work clothes, a dark skirt and white shirt.

"My sis ain't gonna mind," Pa added. "Tell her I said 'hey.'"

The girls looked at each other.

"This here is all your doin'," Betty growled at Ann. "I'm a go, but I ain't gonna have no fun."

"That's because you gots no sense of adventure," Ann snapped at Betty. "'Sides, you just wanna go and pass the time hidin' and kissin'. C'mon, Pee Wee, we can go and have fun."

"Now, Patricia Ann, don't tease," Ma said. "One day, you gonna have a man and think the world of him."

"Not unless he rich," Ann mumbled.

"What was that?" Ma asked.

"Nothin'." Ann stifled a laugh and glanced at Pee Wee, then Betty.

Normally, Ma was the one yelling, but since Pa came home, Ma stepped back and let Pa discipline the girls.

"No sneakin' off," Pa said, his voice filling the room, "and maybe I'll bring back some pralines or somthin'."

He might come across as gruff and stern, but he was soft-hearted, and his rules always came with rewards like pralines, caramels or other sweet bribes.

Ma was in the kitchen area of the room, checking her packed lunch for the girls. She walked over with a cup of black coffee. Ma never liked anything sweet in her coffee. She liked to say, "The blacker it is, the better it tastes." One day, Ann had replied, "Well, it sure must taste delicious cuz it's black as night." Ma didn't think the phrase was funny. Ann had chuckled, but she never joked about Ma's coffee again.

Betty huffed. "Fine! I'll go to Aunt Teddy's. I ain't goin' to like it though."

"I gots to head to town for work. You comin'?" Ma headed for the front door. "Cousin Skeet is comin' by to watch the house while ya'll are gone. I'll pay her two bits to do the laundry and cleanin'." She stopped at the threshold and looked back. "I just want y'all to see what it's like workin' with your aunt for a few days. Don't like it, you can work the fields with Skeet."

Pee Wee and Betty groaned aloud, but Ann ran over and kissed Ma on the cheek. "Thanks, Ma!"

Ma smiled. "Well, tell Skeet to hang out for a few days, in case y'all may be gone longer. I'll pay her a lil extra."

Pa held his arm out for Ma, and they stepped out the front door together.

"See you girls in a few days with pralines," he called back to them. "Fresh pralines! Tell my sister that I sends all my love!"

"Right," Pee Wee muttered under her breath.

After the door was shut, Pee Wee threw a shoe at Ann.

"Whatcha do that for?" Ann picked up the shoe and threw it back.

"Cuz all this was your dumb idea. Ain't askin' us if we had summer plans."

"Pee Wee, you's too young for plans, and Betty almost out the house. If'n anything, she need to finds a man or somethin'."

"That's what I was gonna do 'til you decided my summer ain't important no more," Betty said. "Next time, will it hurt to ask if we wanna do somethin' like this? You know, run it by us before you start talkin' to Ma and Pa, on behalf of us?"

"On *beee*-half of us!" Pee Wee echoed.

A sharp knock at the door quieted them.

"I never asked for y'all to come," Ann snipped. "Ma just decided on *beee*-half of y'all. Be thankful somebody think 'bout you."

Betty opened the door, revealing Cousin Skeet. The warm sunlight shone down on her brown-leather skin. She had one eye and wore a ratty old apron. She liked to laugh loud and clap her hands when she did. She wore her hair in a long braid down her back, and she would always tell everyone she was some part Indian on account of her hair. She shuffled inside with her trademark limp. Whenever asked about it, she claimed that she'd lost a part of her foot in some kind of fight. "That other guy that tried to fight me looked worse," she'd say, snickering, whenever someone looked at her foot.

The girls ran over and hugged her. They weren't sure if Cousin Skeet was really their cousin, or if she was even related, but they loved her all the same.

"Cousin Skeet, you gonna be fine here all alone?" Pee Wee asked.

"Fine and dandy." Cousin Skeet's voice filled the room. "Ma says y'all goin' to work for the 'conjure woman.' If'n you can, ask her for somethin' to fix my feets. I'd be grateful."

"Ann, since this all you, you gets to talk to her." Betty adjusted her shirt. "I ain't into none of this. Rather stay here."

"Well, let's go!"

"Skeet, Ma wanna know if you can stay a few days," Betty said. "All because of Ann, we gotta stay away from home for a bit."

"Y'all goin' someplace else?" Cousin Skeet leaned in and half closed one eye. "Tell ol' Skeet."

"Just passin' time with Pa's sister," Betty said. "Against our will."

"Y'all gonna have fun. Stop all that fussin'! Sides, I ain't too busy. I don't mind. Least your Ma can pay me a bit more. I can go gets my shine from them boys." She leaned back and guffawed.

Pee Wee mouthed, "Shine?"

"Moonshine, idiot." Ann smacked Pee Wee in the head. "For someone that grew up down here, you sure is stupid."

"Your pa is stupid," Pee Wee retorted.

Betty moved the girls apart. "Stupid is as it does, so shut up both of y'all."

"Right. Skeet, we's leavin'," Betty said. "Shotgun behind the door, if'n ya need it. Ma should be back tonight. I think."

Ann pulled closed the door and showed Skeet the shotgun. "Bullets is over by the chair. I's sure you can find 'em."

"Skeet don't need no bullets." She held up her hands like she was going to punch someone, and they all laughed.

Cousin Skeet sat down in the rocking chair, and the girls sauntered toward the door.

"Hey! Girls! Don't call your aunt a swamp rat, okay? She may throw them roots on ya." Cousin Skeet clapped her hands and laughed. "She may throw roots on that lil cute boy that come round lookin' for you, Betty." Her feet flew off the floor as she kicked back and laughed again. Her laugh sounded like something scratching at the door.

"Oooooo, you like Gene!" Pee Wee pointed at Betty. "That's why you don't wanna go with us, huh?"

Betty's cheeks flushed red. "Just shut up and go!"

Ann was the last one out the door. As she pulled it closed behind her, she heard Cousin Skeet mumbling to herself to get cleaning.

Betty led Ann and Pee Wee down a well-worn path. Huge oaks lined the sides of the path, and sunlight dappled the path, showing them the way. Everything was in bloom and seemed to be alive and moving.

"Is it true? You likes that boy?" Ann asked Betty.

"I can say I'm interested. He come to my window night before last. Asked me to take a walk down yonder. I nicely declined." Betty swatted at a bush on their right. "I mean, maybe? I don't know. I can even work in town at they store. Since I can pass, she may get more business. You know, with all my good looks and charm."

"Some of them folk in the city are crazy. It could be a bad idea. Them ol' white men come round and only want one thing." Pee Wee trudged behind them, playing with a twig.

"What them white men want, Pee Wee?" Betty asked. "You don't know nothin' 'bout some birds and bees. And you only ten. Enlighten me."

"Then, lighten me! I'll lighten you!" Pee Wee snapped.

"You only ten, what you know 'bout nothin'?"

"Excuse me, ten and a half!"

Betty waved her hand and dismissed Pee Wee. "Not enough halves."

"Ma say that 'bout you, Gene, and 'that got-damned store'," Pee Wee sassed, upset that her age was always figuring into something.

"Y'all stop it!" Ann interrupted.

The girls walked in silence. The only sound was the wind rustling through the leaves around them. The air smelled like wet grass and wood rot. Pee Wee lagged behind, pausing often to look up at the huge trees touching the sky. She'd walk over, put her hand on a tree trunk, and pretend to listen to it. Betty warned her to watch for the moss around the roots, because that's where the monsters live that take you to hell. Pee Wee laughed it off, but after that she stayed away from the trees.

Ann jumped and screamed when a snake fell off a tree in her path.

"Take one to know one," Betty tossed over her shoulder.

Ann growled.

The further they walked into the forest, the more it smelled like wildflowers.

"Like a skunk," Ann deadpanned.

"Well, them flowers smell sweet, and I imagine they is pretty."

A branch cracked and fell off a tree, crashing down next to the path. They all jumped and then laughed.

"I think ya can hear the trees groanin' when they reach up to the sky," Pee Wee said, craning her neck upward. There wasn't much sound around them, just a few woodpeckers pecking at trees once in a while.

A duck with a line of ducklings behind her crossed their path. They looked like they were trying to find the nearby river. The girls stopped, and Pee Wee squatted down. She ooh-ed and aah-ed at how tiny the ducklings were.

"There's a 'Pee Wee' everywhere. Look at how them lil ducks is waddlin." Pee Wee laughed.

"Careful, don't want a gator to come up from the water and get ya!" Betty pushed Pee Wee a bit.

"You best watch it!" Pee Wee said.

"Well, least we can do is spread the bushes so they can see the water over yonder." Ann leaned down and shifted a shrub to the side for the ducklings to find the water.

They walked on, with Betty leading—until she stopped abruptly and began dancing about on the path. Ann and Pee Wee looked at each other and shrugged.

"I done walked into a spider's web! Dammit, Ann! This is all your fault!" Betty pulled at the invisible webbing on her body and swatted at her face. "Pee Wee, is there anything on my face or back?"

"I kinda don't like spiders, so I'm gonna say no."

"Really? Ann! Can you check? I don't like spiders much either!" Betty twirled in front of Ann.

"Stay still! I can't see much with you moving!" Ann tried to inspect Betty's shirt. She looked up at the leaves blocking the daylight. "There's not enough light under here. We gonna have to go find a field or somethin."

"There's some sun over there!" Pee Wee pointed.

To their left was a thick patch of grass. Dragonflies drifted lazily above it, and frogs croaked on some nearby logs. To their right, they heard something splash into the river.

"Probably ducks," Ann said.

"Well, let's get over there and see." Betty marched off the path and toward the grass.

Ann stepped forward, following Betty, and stopped. "I don't think this is a good idea. My foot is stuck in somethin."

"Oh no!" Pee Wee whispered. "Gators!"

"Please! Ain't no gators down here—" Betty tripped mid-sentence. She stumbled and ran back over to the path. "C'mon!!"

The girls ran behind her, Ann still trying to get the muck off her shoe.

Finally they stopped and leaned over, breathing heavily.

"What was it?" Pee Wee asked.

"I wanna say a gator, but coulda been a log." Betty laughed. "I feel real stupid now."

Ann whacked her shoe against a tree trunk. "And had us running like fools!"

They all laughed and started walking again.

Ann half-jumped down the path, trying to put her shoe on again.

"Ann, is your shoe okay?" Pee Wee asked.

"Good as it get."

"Ya know," Betty said, "when Pa is home, sometimes Ma is real happy. But when he ain't there, she's floating around the place. What is going on? Y'all know?"

"Well, she say he come home rich and go out to the races," Ann said. "Then he come back broke…or somethin'."

Pee Wee perked up. "Y'all think he gots another family somewheres?"

"Dunno," Betty said. "But Pa ain't the smartest."

"Well, it's just when I can't sleep, I think stuff like that," Pee Wee said.

"I'd be sad though," Ann said. "I'd be real sad."

"I know. Man, I loves my pa." Pee Wee swatted lower at the shrubs.

"Nothin' we need to worry 'bout now. He home with us now." Betty faced them. "We smart like Ma and her kin. They always put a little aside. They call it just-in-case money."

Ann put her index finger and thumb under her chin, looking up at the sky. "Ya know, we always got stuff and never do without. I'm not gonna worry 'bout it."

"Let's get to gettin'," Betty said, leading them again. "Looks like clouds rollin' in, but I can't be sure. We should almost be there."

Pee Wee snapped a twig off a bush. "Hey, y'all, seriously, what if Pa runnin' numbers again?"

"I heard Pa's pa was killed gamblin'," Betty said.

"For real?" Ann asked.

"Yup, and how Ma only wanted girl babies cuz she ain't wanna have to send her sons to follow the railroad. Y'all know, lookin' for work like Pa. She say it ain't safe."

"Well, we ain't no safer!" Betty said. "Y'all know Deborah in my class last year? I heard she done already got married an everythin'. Her Ma let some rich white man take her to the city, and she live in a big ol' house on Bourbon Street."

"How is that not safe?" Ann asked.

"I said he was a white man! And besides, no one heard from her since."

Pee Wee joked, "Maybe she got a new face or somethin'."

"Maybe she just in Europe or somewhere," Ann said hollowly.

"Shh! I hear something!" Betty squatted a bit, and the girls pulled in close to her.

Leaves rustled nearby. Someone was approaching. She was singing a melody then switching to talking to herself, as if reciting a list of groceries.

A very tall, dark-skinned woman walked out of the trees onto the path and looked down at them. "I can hear y'all a mile away. Y'all louder than a rooster in an empty hen house. I heard you way back over yonder." She smiled and extended her hand. "Betty, Ann, nice to see you again. I only ever heard of you, Pee Wee."

"Aunt Teddy!" Betty stepped forward and hugged her. "Ann, you was real little when she come round."

"How little?" Ann asked.

"Like a baby little." Teddy stretched out her arms.

Ann hugged her next. "You got a smell like somethin' familiar. I remember this smell. And I heard so much about you. I mean 'sides from Ma callin' you a swamp rat. Skeet say good stuff though."

Teddy hugged her and kissed her on the forehead. "Some things don't change."

"You look like Pa," Pee Wee whispered, "but you a lady."

"He's my little brother and all I got in the world. Now, come give your Auntie a hug." Pee Wee ran and jumped into her arms. "That's a girl."

"Oh, you do smell good." Pee Wee exhaled into her neck.

"A lady has to be unforgettable, remember that." Teddy smiled and placed Pee Wee on the ground. "Now, I gots three beauties for nieces, so I guess I's happier now." She turned, picked up a burlap bag, and started walking. "Y'all comin'? I'm guessin' my brother put up a good enough argument, seein' as your Ma still calls me a swamp rat."

"What else ya know?" Ann teased.

"I know y'all s'posed to stay with me a few days."

The girls looked at each other in amazement.

"She magic," Pee Wee whispered.

"So, what you do?" Ann pushed her way to the front of the line and walked directly behind Aunt Teddy.

"Today I'm out gathering stuff. I gots some work to do for some townsfolk." Aunt Teddy stopped and picked up something, "See, this here onion is for fever. If you got one, you bind it to yourself or somebody, and it'll break the fever right up."

They watched her grab a bunch more onions from the ground, dust the dirt off the roots, and shove them into her bag.

"What else ya got in that bag?" Ann asked.

"A lot of this and that." Teddy set the burlap bag on the ground. She started to pull things out. "I always have my Bible. That's important."

"But you's a conjure woman" Ann furrowed her eyebrows. "Why you got that Bible?"

"I can believe in Jesus and God. This ain't voodoo, child. This here is hoodoo that I do."

Pee Wee pushed forward. "What's the difference?"

"Hoodoo got one God. Voodoo don't." Teddy rooted around in the bag. She grabbed some things and put them on the ground. "These are dried snakeskins and some dehydrated scorpions. I got some brown beer bottles to catch spirits."

Ann squatted, examining a snake. "What's this snake for?"

"Well, I can use it to make goofer dust. I got some sacks of spices in these little bags. And here's some devil grass for blinding someone." She held up a clear plastic bag filled with something that looked like sand. "Dirt from an anthill. I hear if you sprinkle it on food, it makes a person crazy."

"Oh, I wish I had that in school," Pee Wee said under her breath.

"No, ya don't. You too young to cast spells and such." Teddy laughed. "But I'll show you how to gather some stuff for me."

"Is that all we gonna be doin'?" Betty put a hand on her hip.

"If that's all you want to do. If not, don't worry about it." Teddy returned the items to the burlap sack. "I got a feeling that you don't want to be here."

"What gave it away," Betty said dryly.

Ann stood, wiping the dirt from her knees. "I'm sorry for my sister. She just...just...had other stuff to do."

Teddy smiled. "It's okay. I got somethin' for all ya to do." She grunted and lifted the burlap sack on her back. "Can you grab those bottles on the ground? I gotta pick a little bit more stuff before we head back."

Pee Wee grabbed two brown beer bottles, Ann grabbed two more, and Betty tried to step over the others before Ann pressed the bottles in her hands. "Please?"

Betty snatched the bottles and turned her nose up. She sighed and stepped around them to follow Teddy. "Try and keep up, y'all."

Teddy led them. "We gots lots of work to do, so let's get movin'. I got us a chicken and some fresh berries for lunch. Unless y'all ain't ate them hoecakes yet, then you can have that."

Pee Wee stared at her, and then looked at her sisters. "She's ah-MAZE-in'!"

Aunt Teddy laughed. "Lets get goin', lil one. There's a lot involved in learning rootwork. It's not a one-day kinda thing."

Pee Wee was last in line and throwing the biggest questions forward. "Is you a Amazon, cuz I heard they got them in Africa? Cousin Skeet asked if you could make somethin' for her foot too. She limpin' real bad again."

Aunt Teddy turned and looked at Pee Wee. The line stopped. "How bad is she limpin'? Because I don't think I can fix what she got."

Pee Wee spoke up from the back. "What she got?"

"She got that 'ol' lady syndrome'. Her body ready to quit. She keep pushin', and one day she gonna die in them fields. Now, c'mon…idle hands and all that."

They trudged along in silence, with Pee Wee at the back, Betty carrying the sack that contained their food and two beer bottles, and Ann marking the trees with a piece of chalk she'd pulled from her pocket.

Betty looked back at her, eyebrows raised.

Ann grinned. "Don't wanna get lost in the woods, you know?"

Betty snorted and kept walking.

Off in the distance, there was the sound of an animal making a high-pitched hoot.

Pee Wee ran up on Ann. "What was that? Did you hear that?"

Ann stopped. "The sound of you running into me?"

"No…" Pee Wee looked around. "That!"

"It's an owl."

"In the daytime?!" Pee Wee pushed Ann to walk again.

"Yes, in the daytime!" Ann started to laugh. "It's the woods; everything is out everywhere. I mean, look up! We can't even see the sky!"

"Well, this part of the woods don't look so good. It's just a bunch of dead trees leaning on each other and falling. I hope we don't run into another gator."

"Teddy knows the way. I'm sure she ain't gonna kill us."

"Unless I need a body part for some powder or something!" Terry shouted. "We almost there!"

"I rather be at home, ya know," Betty said. "Not in the woods lookin' at these snake-lookin' vines."

"If you lucky, try and grab one," Terry said with a laugh. "I can always use more snakeskin. They not poisonous. I don't think."

Pee Wee groaned. "She a joker like dad."

Aunt Teddy casually reached her right hand out and grabbed something. She inhaled it and dropped it to the ground. "No good."

The girls looked down at the discarded green twisted leaves on the ground.

Ann elbowed Pee Wee. "I dare you to touch it."

Pee Wee stepped on it instead. "She didn't want it. Ain't no good."

As they walked on, Pee Wee paused now and then to look up at the vines hanging from the trees or at insects crawling on the ground. She ran her hand over some moss-covered rocks and watched Teddy pick things to smell or taste. Pee Wee mimicked her, eating some sweet berries and smelling leaves that had a lemon scent.

Ann motioned for Pee Wee to catch up.

"At least we walking toward the sunshine," Pee Wee whispered.

"No owls up here," Ann snickered.

Pee Wee stopped to stare at some rays sliding between the branches, shining down on the forest like spotlights.

"C'mon, Pee Wee, keep up!" Betty yelled.

"I'm getting my bearings so I don't get lost. Ann's map is in her head." Pee Wee waved them off. "Do I need to hurry?"

"Would be nice," Betty said.

"Maybe you want to hurry." Ann's voice was flat, and she was pointing at something to the left.

Pee Wee joined them, and all three stared. The short black-iron gates were twisted and falling apart, and just beyond them were headstones—or rather, there were some headstones, and some mounds of rocks where headstones should be. Further away stood a few statues. Even in daylight, it looked like a bad place. Cemeteries were places you didn't pass in the dark.

Pee Wee looked up at the sky and back down at the headstones and wondered why a cemetery would be out here, hidden in the woods.

"That's where some slaves were buried," Aunt Teddy said, pausing to fix her bag. "We don't use that one for hoodoo stuff. We respect it. Never steal from your ancestors, you gonna be sorry." Her words had a heaviness about them.

"Can I go look?" Pee Wee asked.

"Why? You don't know nobody over there." Aunt Teddy raised her arm and pointed at something off in the tops of the trees. "C'mon, let's get to gettin' while it's good."

They followed Aunt Teddy around a deep marsh with dragonflies lazily drifting above it.

"There it is. My house." Aunt Teddy pointed, but they didn't see anything that even resembled a house. "Look up," she said.

The house was built on stilts high enough that it was almost completely hidden by the tree canopy around it. Leaves rested on the rooftop and fluttered to the ground all around it. Grass grew thick and high around the base of the stilts, and Spanish moss hung from the house like strings of pearls and spiderwebs.

As they drew closer, the girls noticed the short dock that led out to the river. It seemed much wider now than it had earlier, where they had seen the ducks A small rowboat was fastened to the dock. There were two ladders: one directly beneath the house, and another in the front, which Aunt Teddy climbed up, telling them to follow.

The front room was a porch with screens covering the windows and a faded green flower-print sofa. The sickly sweet smell of magnolia and jasmine swirled around the room, and beneath that was a layer of what smelled like wet earth. Baskets and buckets of plants filled the porch, front to back. In a corner was a small table with small jars and red pouches on it.

Ann picked up a red pouch. "You use this to cast?"

"Yep. But be careful. Don't go pickin' nothin' up in anybody house." Aunt Teddy grinned and nodded for Ann to set the bag back.

"Don't touch nothin'!" Pee Wee whispered.

Aunt Teddy tossed the burlap sack she was carrying onto the sofa.

"Let's go inside." She stood in the threshold of the door and waved her hand inside the house.

Initially, the smell was peppermint. Then lavender. Then honeysuckle. Then cinnamon. The smells were intoxicating and came from every part of the house. Plants were everywhere, and if the many shelves on the walls weren't covered by plants or bottles, there were stacks of paper. The papers were filled with sketches of plants and scrawled notes.

The worn, wood floor groaned as they stepped across it.

"You got a cat or somethin'?" Ann asked.

"Cats good for one thing...bones." Aunt Teddy laughed. "I ain't got time to care for one! What I'm gonna do with a cat? 'Sides from boilin' it."

Betty feigned a gag, and they followed Aunt Teddy into the back of the house.

"On the right is my bedroom, and on the left is the kitchen." She walked into the kitchen and sat in a chair in the corner before walking to the kitchen doorway, watching the girls touch several bottles on the shelves. Some were filled with powder, others contained liquid with a creature of some sort floating in it.

"What's this?" Ann asked, holding a jar with some dried dark powder in it.

"Oh, that's 'High John the Conqueror. Watch it." Teddy pointed.

"And what is this?" Pee Wee picked up a glass jar almost as big as her head and turned it around. "Look like a snake or somethin'."

"That is snakeskin. Used for different things."

"Like what?"

"Meh, like puttin' roots on somebody."

"And what's in these jars?" Ann ran her finger over a shelf of short jelly jars filled with different colored powders.

"Well, the first one is lemongrass, then licorice root, lavender, cinnamon, some sage, roses, red salt, white salt, and sulfur."

"Wow, look at this here." Pee Wee shoved her hand into a huge brown bowl filled with bones. "Can't nobody have this many real bones in a house."

The sisters laughed.

"Well now, them's black-cat bones. See, the secret is, ya gotta get a wild cat. They give the best bones and always have the best luck." Aunt Teddy groaned and stood from the stool she sat on. She reached up and pulled down a bouquet of dried flowers. "I'm gonna need for someone to grind these up real good. Smell it."

"Uh, how you kill a black cat?" Pee Wee pushed. "I mean, how you get the bones?"

"I got a pot out back, and one in here. You gotta get the whole cat in and cook it for a long time. It's gotta be alive. No dead cats. Dead cats are bad luck..."

"But if you boil them, you kill 'em, right?" Betty said. "So, it don't matter."

"Well, you gotta know how to boil 'em. I think I gave your pa a black-cat bone on a string. He used to throw them dice instead a goin' to church with your ma. I told him that he best come home with the sweet blood a Jesus, if he was goin' to miss a sermon."

"Did he?" Ann asked.

"Is your ma still with him?" Teddy threw her head back and laughed. Her laugh filled the entire house.

"All right, come on into my room. I got somethin' to show ya."

How this place held up a four-poster bed seemed to defy all physics. On one side of the bed were more pieces of paper with different scribblings, drawings, and writings on them, and a jar filled with writing utensils. On the other side of the bed, on the floor, were several large books half-stacked and half-strewn, with pages marked by different colored ribbons or folded edges. There were even knives in place of ribbons, marking the pages as well. Some had hand-drawn leaves and flowers on the cover. Others were covered with leather and shiny gold letters on the front.

Betty picked one up and thumbed through it. She stopped on a picture of a black cat with different marks on it. "Where'd you get these books?"

"I get 'em from the gettin' place." Aunt Teddy took the book and snapped it closed.

"Where's the gettin' place?" Ann asked.

Teddy laughed, her white teeth shining like pearls against her dark skin. "Why, my dear, that would be next to the shittin' place."

Pee Wee stifled a laugh, and Teddy winked at her. Betty and Ann looked at the floor, their cheeks flushing a bit redder than when they had run through the woods earlier.

"So, we supposed to spend a few days over here cuz Ann wanted to come," said Pee Wee. "What else is we s'posed to do all day?"

Aunt Teddy made a motion for them to sit on the bed. "I was gonna show y'all some easy spells, and how to gather some herbs and stuff."

Ann, sitting on the edge of the bed, tented her fingers. "Where you from? You don't sound like us when you talk."

"Ah, well, I take it since your ma is still callin' me a swamp rat, she ain't tell ya my story."

"Oh yeah, Ma don't like you at all," Pee Wee answered.

Teddy fixed her overalls, tugging up one of the straps that had fallen off her shoulder, then walked into the other room and picked out three bowls, three grindstones, and some flowers.

She gave a bowl to each of them and made a few motions to show her how it was done. The three sat on the floor, grinding, while Teddy stepped out onto the porch to grab the burlap bag.

She returned to the big old armchair in the corner, placed the bag between her spread legs, and started going through it. "How's my brother?"

"He come home and brought us car'mels."

Teddy raised her eyebrows. "Car'mels, you say? Pee Wee, you got taste like a rich white woman."

Pee Wee raised her chin and crossed her arms. "I've been tellin' y'all, I'm supposed to be rich."

"Ma was real happy," Ann said, jumping in. "He went to town this mornin' with her."

"Hmm." Teddy chewed on a blade of grass like a cigarette while she looked through the bag. "He still playin' numbers?"

Betty held her hand out in front her sisters, signaling for them to stop talking. "Not 'til you tell us where you from."

"Well, you got me." Teddy leaned back. "We was born down here in the South, but, somehow we got split up. I think maybe Ma took me up North to get a education, and little Robert— your pa—stayed in the South with my pa to work and send up money for school."

Ann's voice rose from the floor: "Get to the part 'bout hoodoo learnin'! I wanna know how you learnt it!"

Aunt Teddy smiled. She looked away from the girls. "Well, one day I was waitin' for my ma at school, and this lady showed me a trick. I can't remember the trick, but it was a good one.

She told me I could learn them tricks too, but I gots to come to her shop. When Ma showed up, I told her about the lady and the shop, but Ma was not havin' it. Said she knew that lady and told me to stay away."

"Did ya listen?" Pee Wee asked.

"Course not! I snuck over to the shop one day when I's suppose to wait for Ma. I was amazed! Never seen nothin' like it. I walked into the shop and looked around at everything. Didn't say much, just looked. 'What ya need, honey?' some lady asked. I shook my head, like I was a mute. Then, the other lady come from the back and said I was there to see her. I stared at her. She was the lady that showed me the trick. Dressed real strange but smiled like a cat, she did. She led me in the back. I seen some strange stuff back there. Strange."

Pee Wee jumped up, spilling petals on the floor. "Like what?"

"Well, ya got to understand, voodoo is all kinds of stuff… like a gumbo. Goddesses and stuff…and what I saw was some kinda chicken feathers all over the place. There was a woman. She was wearin' all white but had some blood on her. She mumblin' somethin' and look right at me. I like to pee my pants. For the first time in my life, I was scared."

"I know I woulda been," Ann whispered.

Betty asked, "Why ain't you leave?"

"Because that lady had me by the wrist. She was draggin' me somewhere. We ended up in a storage room. She showed me all the stuff round the walls like mockingbird eggs, red devil lye, lizards and things in jars, and these pictures of voodoo saints. She blew somethin' in my face and laughed. I was fallin' all over that room, tryin' to get out. Then, everythin' went black."

"Did she kill you?" Pee Wee gasped.

"She is sittin' right here, so, ah, no," Betty said.

Aunt Teddy laughed. "I was powerful scared. Next thing I know, Ma is standin' over me with fire in her eyes. Oh, she was mad. She also cussed that voodoo lady out and dragged me out that store."

"How she know you was in back?" Ann asked.

"Dunno. She never answered me when I asked. And I asked for a long time. But after that, we moved around a lot. Maw kinda went crazy, sayin' no grass could grow under our feet if we keep movin'. We finally made it down here to the parish. Ma's kin folk live on that other side of this mountain.

"But when we got down here, Ma let go. She just gave up on everything. Like life and stuff. Pa come back with Robert. They made it in time for Ma's funeral. Pa asked if I could stay with Ma's people and he would send money. They said okay, and I was alone again. But they was real good folk. Took good care of me and taught me the ways of hoodoo." Then she spoke through clenched teeth: "I always wanted to go back and get that voodoo bitch. She gone get hers in the end times.

"My brother wrote to me whenever he could. His letters made it sound fun. Him and Pa would hop a train. They worked on railroads with Chinese men!"

"Chinese men?" All three girls asked.

"Uh-huh. 'Til Robert found someone to write for him. He sent me a letter sayin' Pa was killed in some kinda accident. They gave him Pa's money and scraped up stuff for a funeral. Robert said he was comin' back to the parish. Said he met a girl." Aunt Teddy winked. "Y'all's mama. Next thing I know, two of ya was out, and Pee Wee was on the way. Lot of my folks is gone, and it's just me, Robert, and your ma. 'Til your ma found out what I did and said she ain't want no parts of me. I protected y'all though. Just cuz you can't see me, don't mean I ain't there."

"But who taught you hoodoo?" Pee Wee finished with her bowl and set it next to her.

"My ma's folks. They real heavy in it. I learnt from the best in the South!" Aunt Teddy raised her chin and stuck out her chest. "Folks would come see them ladies from far and wide. Even the daddy of the sheriff came, cuz his wife couldn't have no babies. Next thing, she pregnant and he was all happy. He thanked them women and didn't come round no more." Teddy leaned forward. "Tell me 'bout your pa. Still gettin' in trouble?"

Betty snickered. "Yeah, Pa still runnin' numbers. We ask him to stop, but he get on a roll and then he go shoot the dice and come home. He give Ma enough money to keep her happy and to keep shoes on our feet. I'm gonna be goin' to school in town—like, finishin' school—next year. Ann's comin' too, and Pee Wee's gonna finish here."

"And what you wanna do, missy?" Teddy nodded at Ann.

"I wanna learn to do some rootwork with you. I wanna spend my summer here, learnin'."

Teddy nodded her head. "And you, little one?"

"I dunno," Pee Wee said. "I's just out with my sisters cuz ma told me I had to come."

"But your life. Whatcha wanna do?"

"Ain't thought 'bout it much. I's just a kid."

Aunt Teddy looked at Betty again. "I guess you don't wanna be here. I can tell, ya know. Don't lie to me."

"I ain't really interested in none of this stuff—" Betty began.

"I know, but you got a special part in all this. All y'all do. Who can read and write good?"

Betty nodded. "I read pretty good."

"Can ya write?"

"Good enough."

"Good, I need you to take some notes."

"What about me?" Pee Wee pointed to herself.

"When y'all finish with the lavender, I need for you to put these gloves on and go catch me some toads. Not frogs, but toads. They look like the ones by the door, on the second shelf. Get the bucket on the porch."

Pee Wee happily squeaked and jumped up.

Ann was the most enthusiastic. Her mind was set to start weaving spells and putting curses on people...maybe even bringing someone back from the dead. She was upset when Teddy told her to clean the chicken coop instead, despite the assurance that she had something fun for Ann to do afterward.

The three girls worked hard for several hours, until Teddy called Ann and Pee Wee in for some lunch. They trudged up the ladder and lay on the couch on the porch, with Ann leading and Pee Wee in the rear.

"We out here!" Ann yelled to Teddy inside.

"Here is your bag of toads." Pee Wee tossed a heavy burlap sack on the floor and flopped on the floor behind the sack. "I smell like a swamp. I needs a bath, kinda bad."

Teddy came out and set plates on either end of the couch. She now wore a black wrap around her head, making her look regal with her high cheekbones and smooth skin. "Smell means y'all worked hard. Let's have lunch." She grabbed the burlap bag and smiled at Pee Wee. "Nice."

"That smells good." Ann sat up and wiped her hands on her pants. "Who cooked?"

"Go on in the kitchen and wash your hands." Teddy pointed into the house. "I made chicken and hoecakes for lunch. We can pick some fruit for after dinner."

Teddy watched the girls drag themselves to the table. Pee Wee's eyes were downcast, Ann sighed, and Betty barely looked at anyone. Once they sat, they spread their napkins in their laps and started grunting and scarfing down the food. She covered her mouth and laughed a bit.

"What?" Ann said with a mouthful of food.

Pee Wee looked up at Teddy.

"Y'all sound like pigs and eat like men," Teddy said. "Do your ma feed y'all at home?"

"She say we growin'…that's all." Pee Wee picked up a chicken leg and tore into it.

"My Lord." Teddy fanned herself.

When they all finished, Teddy told them they had one more thing to do before they had to start on dinner. She gave them each two bottles, a spade, and a dime.

"We gonna walk up this hill to the cemetery. I wrote names on the bottom of the bottles. Find that grave, go to the foot part, get some dirt from deep, and put it in the bottles. And that's it." Teddy looked at each of the girls. "Okay?"

After they climbed down the ladder, Betty put her bottles on the ground. "I don't know nothin' bout digging in no grave. I mean, ain't that disrespectful or somethin'? I can stay and finish writin.'"

"No, it's not disrespectful. I do what I have to do. This is my job." Teddy picked up the bottles and gave them back to Betty. She adjusted a tan-colored bag with a long strap across her shoulder, putting the full pouch behind her. "You gotta come with us, either way! Child, it's gettin' late." Teddy turned and marched up a hill to the right of her house, beyond the chicken coop.

They walked through a small forest until they reached a clearing with a hip-height wrought-iron fence. The fence formed a square around a cleared patch of land and beyond that were trees that had not been cleared. It seemed as though the trees offered more privacy the further back they were, almost like they were intended to remain there. The entire area was quiet. The air wasn't exactly dead, but it wasn't alive either. There were no flies or crickets, and no grass grew in the area. There was nothing but dirt and gravestones.

Pee Wee looked around and opened her mouth to speak, but Ann shook her head.

"What's goin' on here?" Betty asked. "Why ain't there no sound?"

"Well, I think someone put a spell on the land or somethin,'" Teddy said. "Maybe witches? Maybe Indians. But it's always been real quiet in this one spot."

She made a motion indicating the girls should wait. "Y'all got them dimes, right?"

Each girl pulled a dime out and showed her.

"Sit the dime on the headstone, if'n there is one. If not, put it by the head. On the outside up, not in." She stopped and looked at them. "On second thought, Pee Wee, you come with me. I'm gettin' somethin' off you girl. Like you wanna be here but you not sure. Right?"

"I wanna say 'yeah' cuz it's like an adventure, but I don't wanna make nobody mad."

"Ain't nobody mad at you. Pee Wee," Ann whispered.

"Betty?" Pee Wee asked.

"I wanna go home, but I'm savin' all my anger for Ann." Betty lurched forward and pointed in Ann's face. "I will whup yo ass before this time is over."

"I wanna see you try it!" Ann set the supplies on the ground.

"What in the hell…?" Teddy stood between them. "Y'all tryin' to put each other in the cemetery too? Well, you don't wanna fight over this one. Now get your supplies and do what I done told ya! Put the dimes up, take the dirt, and meet me back here. Me and Pee Wee goin' to the far part of the cemetery. We gots some harder work to do." Teddy grabbed Pee Wee, and they all went through the gate. Newer headstones were near the front, with the older headstones, some crumbling, some gone and replaced with rocks, near the back.

Betty and Ann turned their bottles around and tried to match the names to those on the gravestones. It seemed as though each girl's pair of bottles matched to a pair of people buried near each other.

"Well, is it everythin' you wanted?" Betty huffed at Ann. She jammed the spade in deep and pulled up a clump of dirt.

"And what would we be doin' if we wasn't here? Bent over in a field, pickin' apples." Ann eagerly dug into the ground. She moved with skill and purpose, knowing this was part of a spell that Teddy would have them cast. At least, she hoped. "I mean, we all don't have boyfriends."

"I ain't got no…shut up!" Betty flicked dirt at her.

"Be careful, sis, this work is probably somethin' that'll kill us. You don't know."

Teddy led Pee Wee to the darker part of the cemetery—the area closer to the thick, dense trees that blocked the sun. The ground there resembled scorched earth, but it was covered with small bottles and trinkets. Crickets were fooled and chirped loudly. The earth looked darker than it did in the rest of the cemetery. A few headstones were covered in a thick, heavy moss. Moss tendrils slithered like snakes on the ground, reaching toward the uncovered tombstones.

Teddy carried a small shovel and a plastic bag in one hand and pulled a lighter from her pocket with the other. She flicked the flame and held it out toward the names until she found what she was looking for. Then she dropped her shoulder sack on the ground and pulled a lantern out of it. She lit it and passed it to Pee Wee. "Hold this."

Teddy leaned down and pushed a piece of plastic tarp to the side that covered a deep and half-dug hole.

She stepped down into the hole, jammed the shovel into the dirt, and began digging.

Pee Wee glanced around. Things seemed to be alive and moving in the dirt. Or her imagination took over and she made herself see things slithering and crawling in the dirt. Nervous energy made her jump a bit when she heard Teddy move behind her. "I think there's a snake."

"We outside Pee Wee. Snakes live outside." Teddy grunted and kept shoveling. "I need more light. Come closer. I'm not gonna bite you. And ain't no snakes over here, at least."

"Any snakes over there?" Pee Wee asked, pointing to a random spot.

"Not poisonous ones. I'll tell you what, I'll do somethin' to keep them away." She grabbed some dirt, rubbed it in her hands, and tossed it around the grave. "No snakes are gonna come over here."

"Well, that makes me feel better." Pee Wee relaxed a bit.

Teddy grunted and dug deeper until she could kneel in the hole. Then, she slammed the shovel against something hard and hollow-sounding. "Good."

"Why this person?" Pee Wee asked.

"All these folks was criminals or from prison. Some bad people." Teddy grunted as she worked the shovel. "That's why, when I die, I wanna be buried down low with my ancestors. Don't put me on this hill. Nope."

"Why didn't you drag Ann here with you? She wanted to do all this stuff more than me and Betty."

"Feels like you've got a bigger hunger in you to learn. Could be that you are the youngest and have the most energy." Teddy pointed. "Now, hold the lantern over here more."

"A body ain't gonna jump out the hole or nothin', right?" Pee Wee's hand holding the lantern shook as she leveled it near Teddy.

Teddy glanced at Pee Wee. The way the light from the lantern played on Teddy's face made her look like a demon with hollowed-out eyes and a black hole for a mouth. Pee Wee felt a bit of pee trickle down her leg.

"Better not be pissin' yourself! Now come closer," Teddy hissed.

"Too late," Pee Wee whispered.

Teddy glanced at Pee Wee and laughed. "Now, you can take a bath when we get home. I can't believe you pissed yourself."

"I never said I did!" Pee Wee snapped.

After Teddy finished laughing, she turned and dug a bit more in the hole.

"I'm gonna need you to close your eyes. I know you won't, but there is a dead man's skeleton in here. This here is a sinner-man grave. I gotta get the third rib on the left side."

Pee Wee whispered, "Is that hoodoo strong when you use a sinner-man?"

"Powerful. Can't make nothin' more powerful than with a sinner-man bones." She balanced herself on the edge of the coffin, raised the shovel high, and grunted as she brought it down. The wood gave easily.

Teddy grabbed the lantern from Pee Wee and leaned forward. "Pass me them gloves in the bag."

Pee Wee passed them over. Teddy pulled them on, mumbling, "Smell like nobody loved you enough to do a washin'."

"What's that?" Pee Wee asked. She saw some small bugs or something fly up out the ground in front of Teddy.

Teddy jumped out the hole and crawled around to a different part. She lay on her stomach, reached into the hole and strained as she moved something.

Pee Wee was unaware of the small sounds of fear and grunts of nervousness she was making.

"Quiet, girl! I gotta get this." Teddy huffed. She steadied herself with one black-gloved hand on the ground beside the hole as she bent over it and reached in. "Thank goodness I already had most of this done."

A loud snap cracked the silence.

"What's that?" Pee Wee asked.

Teddy groaned as she pulled herself up out of the hole. "Sinner-man bone."

Pee Wee looked at the bone. Shredded clothing still hung from it. Teddy brushed the dirt and fabric off it and motioned for the bag.

"Now, get some dirt from the foot-part of this grave while I go 'bout fixin' this up." Teddy began shoveling dirt back into the hole.

Pee Wee set the lantern on the ground, took a bottle from the bag, and walked around to the foot of the grave, where Teddy had just rested. She willed herself not to look into the hole, but one of her eyes managed to roll over and look at the bones Teddy was covering. Pee Wee gasped and fell backward.

"Ain't no time for playin'! Come on!" Teddy said.

Pee Wee pulled herself together and slowly scooped some moist dirt into the bottle. She gagged when she grabbed a few worms as well, thinking these same worms had eaten the flesh off the sinner-man.

Teddy looked back and smiled. "Atta girl."

 **BETTY**

I should have fought and stayed at home, but Ma got this thing that all of us sisters need to be together. I think it's one of the numbers she plays because she always snaps at us, "Together with your sisters!"

What is she gonna do when I leave? I wanted to work with Gene and his ma this summer at the store. I need to get acclimated to life in the city. (I've even been studying so I know bigger words, like 'acclimate.') When I go, I ain't never comin' back.

I do wonder, though, if Ma is like that lady we heard stories about—Miss Dot, the one with the runaway daughter. She wanted her daughter to marry someone else, so the girl ran away. Maybe Ma's got somethin' planned for me, or some boy to marry. I hope not. My heart been set on Gene for a while.

Gene is the sweetest. I can't imagine leavin' him behind. I can't imagine leavin' my sisters behind either. But once I leave for school, I think I'm gonna be gone for a long time.

I snuck out one time to go look at the school, and it's a finishin' school for negro girls. They were all dark skin and wore these dresses that looked really heavy. Somethin' about how they walked in a straight line and listened to their instructor made me feel a little more excited.

I took Gene with me to see the school when this man stopped us on our way into town. He was a mean lookin' white man. I wanted Gene to say somethin' to get us outta there, but the whole time Gene was talkin', the man just smiled and looked at me.

Ma told me that I shouldn't be scared of no one except God, but somethin' about this man was off. It was so dark in his eyes that he didn't even need to say a word for me to know he was ridin' the devil's coattails to Hell. He smiled and asked if I knew who he was.

"No, sir."

"Well, I'm the law in these here parts, young lady." He held his hand out for me to shake it, but I didn't move. Everythin' felt wrong. His hand was huge and sweaty.

Gene nudged me, and I leaned forward.

"You're such a pretty young lady," the man said. "You live in the parish?"

"Over yonder, sir."

"You lookin' to make some extra money?" He looked down at me, and I wanted to run from him, but I tried to smile instead.

"I'm in school, sir."

"Whatcha studying?" His voice rattled me to my very soul. I'd need to find a real church and pretend I was Catholic or somethin' to confess. He made me feel dirty with his stare.

This man was not right.

Then someone called Gene's name. When I opened my mouth to speak, a woman grabbed both me and Gene: it was Gene's ma.

"Sorry, Sheriff," she said. "Were they botherin' you? Didn't mean to'. The girl work for me at the store, and this here my son, Gene. He speak French real good." She started pulling us away from him.

"If the lil lady wants to come and work for me, you tell her ma I said she's mighty fine. She can come by whenever. I'll always wait for her."

Gene's ma nodded and dragged us down the street. I think my feet even came off the ground.

She snatched us into an alley and really gave it to us. "Gene!" She slapped him upside the head. "You stupid boy! You done almost got her took by that man! And what I tell you 'bout the sheriff. He like girls like her."

She narrowed her eyes on me. "I know who you is. Ain't your ma and pa told you about that man? How he…how he like young girls like you? How he takes them girls, and sometime they don't come back from wherever? Or they go home half dead with nothin' inside 'em?"

"She told me to mind my own business in town, ma'am."

"You best get to mindin' it. Lord, y'all get home before that fool of a sheriff try somethin'. And I mean it. Don't come back into town unless someone come with ya. Like a bunch of y'all. Many hands can harm, two hands can't do shit." She was a whirlwind of skirts, tearing out the alley and leaving us behind.

I went home and thought about that for a while. It was all I thought about until Ann had to open her big mouth and got me out here digging in dirt. In a cemetery! In the summer! It's too hot, and I'm sweaty. I could whup her ass for volunteering all of us to come and do this! I have no interest in learnin' none of this hoodoo or voodoo or whatever. It's interesting, but if it was such a great job, why can't Aunt Teddy move from the country? She can't ask for payment; it's gotta be donations. I think folks probably offer her anything: food, animals, and maybe even their kids.

That's what I feel like. I'm an offerin' to a hoodoo priestess who has me diggin' in the dirt of dead people.

If I still had my horse, I could ride away from all this. Ride her into town, show that sheriff that he don't scare me none—not if I take my pa's shotgun. I can surprise Gene and his ma at the store, tell them that I can work and need a place to stay. Then she'll show me a room in the back of the store where I can sleep. Gene would visit me, and I would never come back here.

I don't know how I should feel though. Ma wants the best for all us girls. Least, that's what she tells us. She doesn't want us working for no one but ourselves. She said we should be served and not serving. I agree with her. I don't mind if someone sets a plate in front of me, but for me to set a plate in front of a white woman and stand to the side while she eat? No!

I wonder if there's a boy's finishin' school for Gene? That way he can get some class, and we can open our own store or somethin'. I like to dream about the future, me workin' in town with a bunch of white folks coming to see us. I can charge them a little extra for whatever I want.

But I'm gonna have to wait on that. Ann got us out here learnin' some hoodoo. If anythin', I'll learn hoodoo and use it on everybody that get in my way. I'd be blowin' stuff in their faces and blindin' them, bewitchin' them. I'd be able to make all these people do what I want them to do, and then I'll be free.

I'm gonna talk to Gene about his Ma's store when I go back. I deserve more than diggin' in this damn dirt and workin' for a crazy woman with scarves on her head. But Pee Wee and Ann will eat all this up. They follow her around like pups.

I gotta get out of this place. And ain't nobody gonna control my fate and make me do somethin' I don't want to do ever again.

DAY ONE

That night, while the others slept, Pee Wee snuck around the house, looking at and reading everything she could get her hands on. Their teacher always said she was the brightest one in the class, so why not use all them smarts now? She grabbed a book of Teddy's writings they had all taken turns writing in that day and flipped to the page Ann wrote. The words "GOOFER DUST" were scrawled across the top.

As Pee Wee read, she whispered parts aloud: "Hoodoo-ism is goofer dust. Put it in a shoe, and it make you have sore feet or a bad foot. Grind it up—that's called 'conjuration.' Take a snakeskin and hang it where it can dry out. Grind it up, sprinkle over food or in a drink. Now, you puttin' goofer dust inside them, and that make a lot of bad luck."

She paused when she heard someone stir. She picked up the huge book and snuck out to the front porch. When she pushed the door open, the lit end of a cigarette glowed from the end of the couch.

"Figured it'd be you," Teddy said, her voice smooth as molasses. She stared out over the river, not turning to face Pee Wee.

"Figure me what?" Pee Wee closed the book and sat on the opposite end of the couch.

"You got the most curious parts in you. See, Betty, she the logic. She think everything out long and hard before she do somethin'. That's why her and Ann don't get on good. Ann like to go and then think. But you, Pee Wee, you like to plan and watch, then spring into action."

"Like a panther," Pee Wee joked.

She felt Teddy's eyes on her. "Yeah, like a panther."

"So, can I ask you why you got Ann writin' all this down?"

Teddy reached over and grabbed the book. "One day, this book gonna be real important to us. Gonna save lives with it in the future. That time's not yet come to pass. I's the one that gotta get it ready. Me and you, Pee Wee."

"What for you say my name like that? I ain't done nothin but draw toads all day. Catch 'em, cut 'em, and draw 'em. How's that supposed to be important?"

Teddy laughed and took a long drag of her cigarette. "Toads is good for everything. You can use them to cheat at the numbers, like your pa. Write them numbers on a toad belly and let it go. If it jump in front a you, you goin' to win. But ya gotta write them numbers down that you want to win, then bet on 'em."

"Any toad'll jump if you put stuff on they stomach," Pee Wee said with a mocking tone.

"All right, lemme think. Put a dried toad in somebody food, and by the time the tide go up and down, that person will die. Ya gotta put it in the food."

"What else?" Pee Wee asked.

"Ain't you curious at two in the morn? Okay, Pee Wee, lemme think of somethin' good. You can use toads to fix a snake bite. Get bit by a snake? Get a toad, cut it open, and put the open side right on the bite."

"Ugh." Pee Wee groaned.

"Why don't we make somethin' for Cousin Skeet and her rheumatism. I'll let you do it tomorrow and write it in the book. We can make her a soup or somethin'."

Pee Wee shrugged. "I guess she'll like that. It's better than nothin'."

They sat on the sofa and didn't speak anymore until the sound of Pee Wee snoring prompted Teddy to get a blanket and toss it over her.

DAY TWO

On their second day, after a breakfast of beans and rice, Teddy gathered the girls to the front porch and gave them each a bucket.

"Fill 'em up."

"With what?" Betty asked.

"Pee. Pee in them buckets all day." Teddy smiled at the looks on the girls faces. "Oh, you ain't never worked them brothels, huh? They ask you to do even more strange stuff. We not goin' too far from the house today. I need all your pee in them buckets, please." Teddy sat on the couch, one long leg draped over the other in denim jeans.

Betty glared at Ann. "I swear on all that's holy, I'm a beat yo ass when this is done."

"I wanna see you try!" Ann set her bucket on the floor. "Cuz you ain't never done it before, and you ain't gonna do it now!"

Pee Wee felt the hostility growing between them, like two firecrackers with their fuses tied together. "Ann, let's go out and slop the pigs or somethin'."

Ann snatched her arm from Pee Wee's grip. "Ain't no damned pigs to slop."

"Let's just go outside then." Pee Wee stood between them. "Please."

"This ain't over, you!" Ann raised two fingers and pointed at her own eyes, then at Betty.

"That mean you can see or somethin'? You as dumb as the day is long." Betty picked up her bucket and walked in the opposite direction and into the house.

"Lemme go. I'm a go for a walk." Ann stomped across the porch and climbed down the ladder with her bucket, mumbling to herself.

Pee Wee went to follow her, slinging her leg over the ladder.

"You always jump in between them two?" Teddy asked from the couch.

Pee Wee stopped. "None of this started 'til we come here. Now they's like dogs and cats all the time."

Pee Wee watched Ann fume around the chicken coop for a while.

"Ann, you okay?"

"Look like I'm okay? Sure, Pee Wee. Right as rain!" Ann snapped.

"Was just askin', is all." Pee Wee grabbed her bucket and walked away.

Later, after she calmed herself a bit, Ann walked up on Pee Wee digging in the mud for catfish. "Whatcha doin'?"

"Tryin' to catch lunch. Why you talkin' to me? Ain't you gotta go yell at Betty again?" Pee Wee slapped the mud. "Dammit! Got away!"

Ann sat on a rock near Pee Wee's mud hole. "Yeah, sorry 'bout all that. I dunno what's goin' on with her."

"Well, she need to go or you need to go. We only got today and tomorrow here, and I aims to come home knowin' somethin'." Pee Wee picked up a catfish, whacked it, and put it in a burlap bag. "Teddy got a cons-consula…constipat-shun…this afternoon."

"A what?"

"You know, somebody comin'. We gotta sit in the back and listen to how it goes." Pee Wee busied herself with the catfish again.

"Consultation! Oh, okay. What's that all 'bout?" Ann took her shoes off and cuffed her pants. She joined Pee Wee in the mud. "How many ya got?"

"Maybe three. Maybe four. Just started."

Ann's hand dove into the mud and picked up a catfish. "You peein' in that bucket?"

"I feels right dumb, but yep. What she gonna do with it?"

"Well, I may hurt someone, I may cast with it," Teddy said from behind them. "I just can't make enough for what I gotta do."

Ann and Pee Wee whipped around to face her. Pee Wee grabbed Ann's arm, then apologized.

"You scared us!" Ann said.

"Probably scared the last catfish away too." Pee Wee slapped at the mud.

Betty stepped out from behind Teddy. "Sorry, sis, I ain't mean to make ya mad. Aunt Teddy told me how I shouldn't take ya for granted." She set her half-full bucket down. "Y'all need help catchin' catfish?"

"She sure filled that bucket mighty quick," Ann said, nudging Pee Wee.

"Whatcha think that mean?" Pee Wee asked, attacking another catfish.

"Mean she full of it. Come on and help us then!" Ann threw a bit of mud at Betty.

"Actually, I'm gonna need Betty to get some plastic and dirt from over there for me." Teddy pointed. "Off'n that anthill."

"This for today?" Betty asked.

"Yeah, she come by later but not at night. Spirits is out tonight. Not a good night to travel." Teddy walked toward the house. "C'mon, Betty, come get this plastic."

They cleaned themselves while Teddy made lunch with the catfish they had caught. Betty even volunteered in the kitchen and made cornbread while Pee Wee and Ann swept the house clean. When they sat at the table to eat, lunch was well deserved. They shared in laughter as they tried to figure out what the buckets of pee were for—and no one guessed right.

After they ate, Teddy made them sit in the bedroom with the curtain pulled closed and told them that only one of them could be the assistant today.

"On account of what?" Pee Wee sassed and fell back onto the bed.

"On account of I don't need everybody knowin' 'bout y'all. Then, they goin' to come to your house and ask you to cast, and you can't do that." Teddy wrapped the black scarf around her head and pulled the front up, making it look regal as she fastened it in the back. "Who's it gonna be?"

"Rock, paper, scissors, throw!" Ann yelled.

Pee Wee threw rock. Ann and Betty threw scissors.

"Rock crush scissors. Pee Wee, let's get you dressed." Teddy grabbed Pee Wee off the bed and barked orders: "Betty, you wanna cast right? Write this down and get it all together for me before she get here: there's a bottle in the kitchen with the label 'Sinner's Dirt Heart.' That dirt come from a grave over a sinner's heart. Anyway, get that, and the bottle of sulfur, and the bottle of red pepper. Tie a scarf round your face; you don't want to inhale none of this. I call it 'From the Well to the Grave.'"

Betty jumped up and hurried to the kitchen, where she began clanking around.

"Ann, I gots two pots out back. One got black-cat bone and the other got some toads boiled down. I need you to put some grease in the pot with the toads. Mix it good then put it in a jar and bring it up to the kitchen."

"What's it for?" Ann tossed an apron outside the open window.

"I think somebody put somethin' on this gal comin'. She gotta use it a few days to get the spell off of her. Now, y'all knows some spells. Ann, don't forget to write it in the book, okay?" Teddy busily wrapped some lightweight cotton fabric around Pee Wee. She fixed her hair under a black scarf and made her take her shoes off. "Now go check the change bucket by the front door to the porch. Take all the money out of it and put it where I showed you."

Pee Wee nodded and ran to the front door that led to the porch.

By the time Teddy walked out onto the porch, lighting a cigarette, Pee Wee had already put the money away. "She comin' soon," Teddy said. "I see her not far from here."

"Can you really see her?" Pee Wee asked.

"I gotta piece of somethin' of hers. If I focus, I can see her comin'. It's that gift of bein' a real hoodoo priestess. Them fake ones don't have the vision. That's how ya know."

Pee Wee made a mental note and filed it away. "All the money is put away. Ann is downstairs yellin' about the odor, and Betty got everythin' ready in the kitchen."

"Good, cuz she comin' now." Teddy pointed off to the left, past the chicken coops and forest.

A small brown woman glided down the path. She wore her hair pulled back with a black scarf. She had on a brown dress, a black belt, and boots.

"All right, I'll get her. Tell Ann to hurry up. Grease ain't gonna kill her. Smell like stank on a skunk though." Teddy rushed over to the side of the porch and looked out the window.

Teddy walked the young woman into the house. "Have a seat there on the couch, Stella," she said to her.

The young woman stood and wiped at her nose, crying.

Pee Wee ran through the house and yelled out the back window, "She here! Ann, you ready?"

Ann was doubled over on the ground, but she gave a thumbs up. "Tell Betty to come get the grease. I knocked over them black cats and I'm 'bout to be real sick."

Betty laughed. She climbed down the ladder to the backyard where Ann stood, looking sick.

Teddy gently placed a hand on Stella's shoulder and sighed. "Stella, what's the problem?" she asked in a soothing voice.

"Well, I likes Cotton," the girl said, "but his ma don't like me. I mean, I works hard, ya know? I try to help out with they

cookin' and stuff, but no matter, I ain't good enough for him."
She began crying into a handkerchief.

"Ahh…and this other boy? Delphonse? What he do?"

"I think he had someone put a spell on me, cuz all this ain't
start 'til I was tryin' to see Cotton. It's like all my luck changed o
somethin'. I hear you's the best, Miss Teddy! Help me, please!"

"Ain't Cotton the sheriff's kin? He favor him a bit in the face."
Teddy stood and crossed her arms on her chest. "You gotta tell
me everythin', Stella. Not the good parts."

"Yeah, they kin," Stella whispered.

"And you want my help to get these roots thrown off of you?"
Teddy asked.

"Miss Teddy, I just want Cotton," Stella whined. "I knows he
want me too!"

Teddy stepped back and thought for a few minutes. "How
old are both of y'all?"

"Sixteen. That's old enough down here." Stella's voice was
animated. "We can get married and everythin'!"

"Calm down. Just askin'."

Pee Wee watched Ann and Betty scooping the cat grease
before she slipped onto the porch and hid on the other side
of the curtain in the bedroom. Her sides hurt from laughing
at the two of them. She glanced between the curtains and saw
Teddy motion her head toward the bucket.

Stella jumped up, walked over to the bucket, and dropped
some money in. She sat again. "I gave you all I got. Can you
help me?"

"Honey, I's the best there is. But, the sheriff…that's a whole
'nother thing." Teddy frowned and bit the inside of her cheek
before speaking again. "Now you got that swatch of a dress
from Miss Lady? We take it one thing at a time."

"Cotton's mom? Yeah, right here." She reached into a pocket
and pulled out a square of powder-blue cloth and set it on the
table. She let her fingers linger on the cloth. "Is you sure it's
gonna work?"

"I's the best. Trust me, and trust the rootwork." Teddy beckoned Pee Wee forward to take the cloth. "Give this to Betty, and tell her to sprinkle a lil of that stuff in it. Tell her to seal it up and make it nice."

Pee Wee started to walk away but Teddy called out, "And bring me back a jar of that grease." She turned back to Stella. "This my niece, Hattie. She gonna make sure everythin' all right. Now, you gotta listen and do what I say for this to work."

Pee Wee disappeared behind the curtain. She gave Betty the cloth and watched her fill it with some herbs she'd already assembled, reading off a piece of paper she had on the table. Ann was cleaning the residue of grease off the jar and tightening it. When they finished, they gave everything to Pee Wee.

"Don't drop it," Ann whispered.

"I won't!" The jar was still warm, and it smelled like fresh earth and something else. She walked back through the curtains and set the jar full of clear grease on the table. Stella wore rose oil, and it wasn't blending well with the greasy toad-and-cat mix.

"Take a dab a day for nine days, rub it on your arms, and wait 'til after the tenth day. Then go see Cotton."

Pee Wee passed Teddy the small powder-blue bag.

"Meanwhile, drop this in the well on his momma's property," Teddy said. "I know Cotton don't like to drink from one of the wells. It's by the horses. Drop this in there. Don't let nobody drink from it for two hours. She be dead soon enough, then the spell on the bag wear off, understand?"

Stella looked at the jar and the cloth on the table, tears streaming down her cheeks. "I understand. When his ma's gone, he gonna love me like he should."

Teddy grabbed Stella's wrist. "Be sure this is what you want, Stella. You don't know how powerful love spells can be. He will love you to the ends of the world. You goin' to have to come back for another consultation 'bout the Sheriff. That's more rootwork."

Stella sniffled and nodded her head. Pee Wee ran in the kitchen and grabbed a large cloth. She stepped between the curtains and wrapped everything up in it. She gave the knotted cloth to Stella.

Stella thanked her and Teddy several times before she left.

"How we know if it work?" Pee Wee asked.

"She come back if it don't work. Trust me, it'll work." Teddy smiled. "And y'all did real good to not have no home trainin'. I'll split this all with the three of y'all."

Pee Wee's math told her they were all getting five dollars each. *Better than havin' zero dollars*, she thought.

DAY THREE

They rode three horses: Teddy and Betty rode by themselves, and Pee Wee and Ann shared a horse. Pee Wee wrapped her arms around Ann's waist and held tight. She didn't like riding horses. She always preferred to run. At least she could slow down and look at things when she ran. The horse moved so fast that everything was a green blur passing her by, and twigs felt like switches on her skin. She didn't like it one bit.

Betty was always the best with horses, and it seemed like she could talk to them and calm them down. She talked about a time when she had a black horse she named Midnight. The horse was so dark that when it ran at night, people thought a spirit was coming for them. Midnight's hooves sounded like a train running between the trees. And Betty would sit on it's back, with her skin looking pale in the moonlight, and cackle. At least until she was caught in town, skipping school with some friends. Then Ma found the cigarettes on Betty, and Midnight was a thing of the past.

When Pee Wee had first tried mounting the horse, it had shied away from her.

"You can't be afraid of it," Betty had said. "It senses your fear. You gots to get on with confidence." She held the reins and whispered to the horse, pressing her forehead against the horse and caressing its face. "See, soft like this."

"Like a horse can hear you," Pee Wee mumbled.

Ann laughed and climbed onto the horse. She grabbed Pee Wee's arm and helped her mount. "Careful, you in the presence of three powerful gals and one powerful lady. You don't know what that horse can hear."

As they rode through a few small camps in the woods, she smelled many delicious things like hoecakes and bread. She thought she saw pigs being slaughtered out in the open in the backs of some of these homes—big, fat, pink things hanging from hooks with men around them—but maybe her mind was just playing tricks on her. She didn't like the thought of the pigs, and shut her eyes.

It was the smells of the forest that she loved the most: jasmine, honeysuckle, and the sweetness of summer. She focused on the lazy summer day while the horse trotted past the people.

"All right, we here," Teddy said. She dismounted and gave the reins of her horse to a man wearing a huge tan hat and overalls.

"Is he mixed?" Pee Wee asked Ann.

"Look like it. Why ain't ya pay attention this morn when she was tellin' us what we was gonna do today?" Ann jumped off the horse. Then she helped Pee Wee dismount.

The girls looked around the settlement. The locals lived right on the edge of the swamp. No one wore shoes, and everyone seemed to have tan-colored skin, freckles, and curly hair. Their clothes—dresses, overalls, shirts, and pants high above the ankles—were varying shades of blue and all looked a bit ragged.

"They kinda all look the same to me," Ann said.

"I heard of these folks before," Betty said. "We talked about different settlements in class. Mu...Mu-lah...toes. They white family don't want 'em, and they black family don't know 'bout 'em. So, they kinda settle near swamps and stuff."

"Hey, y'all, look-it!" Pee Wee pointed to a few sheds that looked more like lean-tos. They were painted bright blue with symbols drawn on them in black. If the sheds weren't painted blue, they'd blend in behind low-hanging branches of trees and stacks of logs.

"Barely look like somebody live here," Ann whispered.

"And we gotta get over with Teddy. She may got work we can do," Betty said, and turned to Ann. "You got that bag she packed?"

"Sure, let's go."

Betty and Ann walked over and joined their statuesque aunt, who was speaking with someone who seemed to have authority. He was not a tall man, but he exuded an aura of power. His skin was a darker tan than everyone else, and he wore shoes and a dirty white shirt, rolled up to his elbows, and heavy dark-colored pants. He pulled a hat off his head and kneaded it in his hands in front of him as they talked.

Teddy wrapped her hands around his and nodded while he spoke. Soon, he stopped fidgeting with the hat.

All the local women stood back and hid in the woods. Some children played with a rope and a stick, but they were quiet.

Pee Wee noticed a little boy away from the others, playing all by himself near a shed on the edge of the settlement. She tiptoed over to him. He was using a stick to make drawings in the dirt.

"You so tiny, like a doll baby," she said.

"Hi!" The little boy looked up at her. "I'm Isaac."

"Hi, Isaac. I'm Pee Wee." She couldn't believe she had to kneel to talk to him. "Whatcha doin'?"

"Waitin' for my momma. She doin' laundry. It's just me and her. I had a dog, but it gone." He kept drawing. "Sometimes my daddy come round, but not a lot."

Pee Wee thought he was dressed strangely for a little boy. He wore a black suit and no shoes, but his suit wasn't dirty, despite him squatting and playing in the dirt.

She looked around and saw Teddy, Betty, and Ann rushing toward her. The man followed behind them. Pee Wee glanced back at Isaac, who smiled at her before he got up and ran around the side of the shed.

"Hey! What is you doin'? You s'posed to be with me." Teddy's face looked angry, "Beaux, this is my other niece, Pee Wee."

"Oh, chéri, what she lookin' at?" the man asked. He sounded funny when he spoke, like a heavy accent of something. "Hello," he said, stepping forward and extending his hand.

Pee Wee smiled and shook it. "Where you from?"

"My *famile* is from France. We just live down here for a little while." He glanced at Teddy before bending down to speak to Pee Wee. "What made you come over here to this shed?"

Pee Wee looked into his green eyes. His wavy hair looked so soft. She stretched her hand out and asked to touch his hair. He nodded, and she ran her hand through his light brown curls.

"Your hair is so soft. Like *real* soft...kinda like them Cajuns' hair."

Beaux smiled. "Why'd you come over here, Pee Wee?"

"I likes your accent. You sound like a dad." She pulled her hand back and shoved it into the pocket of her overalls.

"Why can't you answer him?" Ann's voice sounded angry. "He done asked you twice!"

Pee Wee looked at all of them and shook her head, like she had something in her ear. She gritted her teeth and covered her ears while closing her eyes. "Huh? Why don't I what? I feel like I can't focus or somethin'. Like it's a bunch of folk talkin' round here, over there and in them trees." Pee Wee pointed out the other people. "And Isaac done ran behind the house and started banging stuff. He real loud like playin' a drum or somethin'."

Teddy's face went blank, and her sisters stared wide. Beaux coughed on his words.

"How many people ya see, Pee Wee?" Teddy asked.

"Uh..." She counted. "Four...eight...eleven. They's eleven people.

Teddy swallowed hard. "You sure?"

"Maybe y'all need to get some water or somethin', I'm not lyin'," Pee Wee sassed and smirked. "I'm tellin' y'all what I see and they over there! All them over there—a momma and three kids, some twin girls like Betty's bad friends, two boys, and a ol' lady with a man by the water, and a baby." She pointed, then she laughed. "Oh, and Isaac. Y'all want me to get Isaac?"

Betty stepped forward. "Yeah, go get him. Where he at?"

"Round back of this shed. Right here." She ran off.

"Beaux, how many people live here?" Teddy whispered.

"They's just three families: me and my wife and kids; Eugene and his wife and they baby girl; and the newlyweds, Anne and Rufus." Beaux turned and pointed out some sheds that were more huddled together than the others. "These people dead and gone a good while. They was some of the first here, and then they was gone."

Ann covered her mouth. "She seein' what?"

"Spirits," Beaux said.

Teddy leveled her hands. "Don't—"

Pee Wee ran back around the shed. "He said to come inside. He don't got a room. He and his momma just got one big room in here."

Beaux followed Pee Wee. She pushed the door open, but it snapped shut in their faces. He reached up and opened the door. "There's a bump here. Watch your step."

They stepped inside and immediately smelled roses and dried flowers. Dried sage hung over the door and garlands of mint were hung around the room. The shed was one large room with a fireplace, some shelves with dishes, and, to the right of the door, two beds. In the far corner was a rocking chair with folded quilts on top of it, and a small table with a vase of dried flowers. Here and there were scattered blocks that Isaac probably played with. On the floor were a pitcher and basin and bags of flour and grains.

"C'mon, boy! My aunt wanna see you. Sure, I'll hold your hand." They watched Pee Wee reach out and grab something.

Teddy froze, and Ann grabbed Beaux before she knew it, and Betty fainted.

"Pee Wee! What in the world is you doin'?" Teddy shouted.

The shape of a boy had appeared.

"Oh Lord have mercy on our souls," Beaux whispered.

"What? What?" Pee Wee looked around.

"Can you tell Isaac we are all happy to see him?" Teddy asked.

"Why can't you tell him? He right here."

"We just want you to tell him for us," Teddy said gently. "He's a kid and maybe scared of us."

Ann released Beaux so he could scoop Betty up off the floor. He put her on the larger bed in the corner and motioned for Ann to go get something for her.

Ann rushed to the corner of the shed where a bucket of water sat. She grabbed a cup, scooped some out, and ran back over to Beaux.

He held the cup to Betty's lips and gently touched the side of her face.

"I'll go get some fresh water somewhere. Don't know how long that been sittin'." Ann rushed out the door and ran into a woman holding a bucket of water, almost causing her to drop it.

"Excuse eh moi," she said and righted herself. Her accent was heavier than Beaux's.

"Is that fresh water?" Ann asked. "My sister need some. She kinda fainted."

"Oh, hey, cups are inside."

"Sorry, who is you?"

"I live here." The woman's tone hardened. "And you?"

"I...uh...I'm here with the hoodoo lady."

The woman mumbled something, set the bucket down, and smoothed her dress. "I'm Rose. Nice to meet you. Would you like to..."

"Miss Lady, what is you doin'? You gonna have to leave!" Ann took the bucket of water. "But I can take this inside, and I'll be right back, promise."

Rose looked astonished, but she sat on a little stool outside the door. "*D'accord*. Okay."

Beaux stepped outside and made a motion for Ann to go back in to help. He spoke to Rose in French, but with a sense of urgency.

Betty sat up on the bed. "What the…I ain't never…"

Pee Wee was still holding the boy's hand, looking confused. "I don't understand how I can see him and y'all can't. He right here. I got his hand. And maybe he want y'all to see him now."

"We can see him when you touch him, Pee Wee. Otherwise, we can't see him at all." Teddy stepped forward and kneeled before him. "Can you hear me, Isaac?"

Pee Wee said, "He nod his head like yeah."

"Isaac, you know that…you don't…you aren't…" Teddy struggled with her words.

"They think you're dead," Pee Wee said. "That's what they tryin' to say."

Isaac looked up at Pee Wee and smiled. "I know. But Momma is so sad when I go. That's why I come back. Then Daddy gone. Momma sad and cry all the time."

"Maybe you ain't supposed to stay," Pee Wee said. "Maybe you can find your dad or somethin'."

"If I leave, Ma gonna be sad and cry." He looked toward the doorway. "She outside right now. I can hear her cryin'…again. It make me hurt *here*."

He pointed at his heart…or where his heart would be.

"I don't know what to tell ya," Pee Wee said. "I mean, if my ma was alone and I was gone, well, I guess I'd be sad too. But I know I'd make more friends and see my ma again soon. We learnt at church that when you die, you goes to this place where the outside is like gold. And all your friends and family is there, and nobody say your hair too nappy or call you a nigger cuz it's a place with nothin' but love." Pee Wee paused. "Oh and the most important part?"

"What?" Isaac's eyes widened.

"Ya gets to meet Jesus and tell him thank you for dyin' for our sins and stuff. And you know what else? Ya never hungry, and ya get to eat all them sweet car'mels and pralines you want."

"For real?" Isaac asked.

"Yup. But if'n you stay here, well, your Ma gonna be sad, and all your family in heaven gonna be sad, and all your new friends gonna be sad. Everybody want you to do this and that, but up there? Ya do whatcha want. And I tell you, when I go, I's gonna put my feet up and eat all the car'mels 'til my teeth fall out. But they won't."

"Why?"

"Cuz I'm in heaven, and it's only good stuff up there. Plus, I need for you to go up there an look for some kids. This girl name Sassy felled into the river last year after a flood. And I told her that I hated her cuz she kept callin' me ugly and stuff. I even hit her in the face…"

"But she wasn't nice? That's okay."

"No. Cuz my ma said I shoulda 'turned the other cheek and forgave that girl, cuz she don't know what she sayin'. Then, I seen her ma cryin', and I remember when we had fun before…and this one time, she took these berries off the bush behind the school. We was outside hidin' cuz we had a nice day. And with the sun and them berries, day was so sweet, and I said to her, 'This right here is heaven. I knows it, cuz everythin' feel happy.' And she said, 'Yeah.' So, after that, I couldn't be mad, cuz maybe she was not havin' a good day or that. But I always wished I coulda said thanks for gettin' them berries and spendin' that day with me."

"You got in trouble?" Isaac asked.

Pee Wee laughed. "Oh, Ma whupped my tail. I mean, I know'd I was wrong, but then when she died, Ma hugged me for so long and told me to thank 'bout the good times. Not the bad."

"And what happen?"

"Then I met my aunt, and today, I met you. And I think it's a sign that you gotta go see her for me and tell her that I'm sorry."

"Can I say bye to my ma? She so sad."

"Your ma gonna be fine. I promise. She got Mr. Beaux and all them other folks here to make her happy." Pee Wee took both his hands. "Let's say bye to your ma, and then you gonna look for *who*?"

"Your friend…Sassah…Sassy, and tell her you're sorry." Isaac smiled.

"Okay, good. Let's getcha ma in, and then you go. Hey, do it look like a white light or somethin'? The thing ya lookin' for. I hear it's a white light, maybe some gold sun rays."

He looked over his shoulder, out the back door. "No. Look kinda like I'm walkin' through the woods, but this lady is standin' and waitin' for me. She so purty. She look like my ma, but older."

"Maybe that's your granny? She got on white?"

"Yeah, and big wings." Isaac smiled. "I was scared of her cuz she just smile, but she say it's okay."

"Then you gotta go. I know my sisters wouldn't wait that long for me."

"Hey!" Ann and Betty yelled.

Pee Wee glanced at them. "It's true!"

"I'm gonna bring his ma in here, okay?" Teddy said. "She gotta say bye, but ya gotta hold his hands for her to see him. It's like you are a conduit…like a special person. We see him through you, but you let go and we don't see him. And ya gotta tell him he gotta go. Does he understand?"

Isaac nodded.

"He say yeah."

Rose stepped inside, and, when she saw Issac, she dropped to her knees and cried. Her plain indigo shirt and skirt were askew.

Isaac tried to pull away, but Pee Wee gripped his hand tighter.

"I wanna go hug my ma!"

"Okay, but I gotta hold your hand. I think that's the only way they can see you!"

"Okay, Pee Wee." They walked across the room. "Hey, you sure is smart."

"I know. I tell my sisters I'm smart, but they don't listen."

"They just wanna be smart too. That's all."

Pee Wee laughed.

They stopped in front of Rose, who cried as she reached out to hug Pee Wee.

Pee Wee pulled Isaac in, and they all hugged. Rose sniffed at Isaac's hair and said things to him in French. He giggled a little until he pulled back.

"Mama, I have to go now," he said. "Mama! I love you."

Pee Wee repeated it.

Rose nodded her head. "I love you so much."

Pee Wee dropped Isaac's hand and walked to the back door of the shed with him. She saw a clear path into the woods and a bright light at the end.

"Do you see her? You see my granny?" Isaac started to run down the path.

"Isaac, all I see is a white light. Run and hug your granny, and don't forget to tell Sassy!" She waved at him as he ran down the path.

He turned and waved to her one last time. "*Merci!*"

Pee Wee turned back to the doorway. Betty and Ann stood with their arms crossed, while Teddy spoke to Beaux and Rose behind them. Betty's brows furrowed, like she was angry while Ann's face was bright with a huge smile crawling across her lips.

Pee Wee sashayed over to her sisters and whispered, "He told me I was real smart. And y'all can't see him, but he say y'all wanna be smart too."

"You's a liar, and that boy a ghost." Betty wagged her finger in Pee Wee's face. "He don't know you like we do. I'll bet this all Teddy's doin' anyway."

Ann laughed. "One person said you's smart, Pee Wee, but he like half a person, anyway."

"You always see spirits?" Betty asked.

"This the first time."

Betty raised her eyebrow. "You messin' with some stuff at Teddy's?"

"I felt this in my pocket, but I'm not sure what it is." Pee Wee pulled out a small white bone from her pocket.

Teddy walked over and picked it from her hand. "Well, what you doin' with a black-cat bone?"

"Aw, you done touched a dead cat," Ann said, laughing.

"Y'all, this bone don't got nothin' to do with her seein' spirits," Teddy said. "Maybe it's the land, maybe she was born with a caul...maybe..."

"What's a caul?" Pee Wee asked.

"It's a piece a skin that cover your face. Maybe you been seein' spirits but you didn't know until today cuz we told you." Teddy smiled. "Looks like I gots me two hoodoo princesses, huh? One to see spirits, the other to throw spells."

Pee Wee and Ann laughed.

Betty crossed her arms. "I'm tellin' y'all, I'm destined for better things. Y'all can come to me when ya done with all this hoodoo."

Ann chuckled. "Yeah, and I'll be right outside your door with a bucket a pee for your mother-in-law."

"Well, this all I had planned for the day," Teddy said. She folded something and put it in her pocket. "Didn't think it would go so quick. Let's get back and getcha ready to go home. I'm sure y'all excited to leave."

"I could stay a whole 'nother week!" Pee Wee said.

"Betcha ma miss you though. Go on home and come back later. I always got stuff to do."

Rose pulled a small handkerchief from her pocket and gave it to Pee Wee. "This was Isaac's. Now, you keep it." She pressed it into Pee Wee's hand.

"Aw, I don't wanna take it from you." Pee Wee tried to push it back.

Beaux reached down and closed his hand around Pee Wee's hand. "Please."

Pee Wee nodded her head and took it from Rose. Rose and Beaux thanked them several more times as they all left the shed.

While Betty got the horses ready and showed Ann how to calm them, Teddy pulled Pee Wee aside.

"I didn't know you could see spirits." She passed Pee Wee a folded bill. "Here's a lil extra."

"Oh, thanks. But can I split this with my sisters?"

Teddy leaned back. "Why?"

"Well, we all kinda came together, and I don't want them mad at me or nothin'. It's all of us."

"You got a good soul, kid, I'll give ya that."

Pee Wee slipped the bill back into Teddy's hand.

"So be it."

THE INCIDENT

Betty and Ann teased Pee Wee the entire way to their cabin from Teddy's.

"Is there one over there?" Ann pointed to a cluster of trees.

Pee Wee sucked her teeth and walked ahead of them.

"Watch out! You might step on a toe of one or somethin'!" Betty elbowed Ann.

Pee Wee grumbled and kept her head down, eyes focused on the worn trail in the dirt that led to their home. She didn't hate seeing ghosts. She thought it made her special. Maybe Pa would love her even more than Betty and Ann when he heard.

"When I get home, Pa goin' to have me some pralines," Pee Wee shouted back at them, "and when I tell him what happened, he ain't gonna give y'all none! Y'all keep teasin' me, and I may calls up that ghost by the willow tree. That lady that hung herself...y'all know." Then she took off running down the trail.

Betty and Ann gave chase, all three of them laughing as they neared their village.

Ma and Skeet were sitting on the porch, smoking pipes. The girls ran over and sat at their feet.

"Ma, you'll never guess what happened," Betty began.

"Pee Wee saw a ghost," Ann finished, "and she sent it on."

Ma looked at Pee Wee, who sat close to her feet. "Is that true, baby?"

"Well...I mean...kinda..." Pee Wee stammered.

"Looks like you got your own hoodoo gal here," Skeet said. "And on that, I will see y'all later. Thanks for the pralines, Ma." She stood and grabbed a cane.

She gripped each girl's shoulder as she stepped around them and down the stairs. "Y'all don't move. Ol' lady comin' through. I can make it. No, don't move now."

Ma laughed. "Move for Skeet, y'all. Act like ya got some home trainin'."

The girls helped Skeet down the few stairs.

"Skeet, uh," Ann said, "Teddy said you need to come see her cuz she ain't got nothin' for ya. Maybe I can take ya over—"

The sound of men yelling interrupted her. They turned to look at the longer path that led to their village, where a pack of men chased another man, who ran, stumbling, ahead of them. He hunched over and moaned as he ran, one hand covering his side, bright blood dripping between his fingers.

No one spoke until Ma jumped to her feet. "Pa? Pa? Is that you?" She pushed the girls aside and half-ran down the road toward him.

Skeet leaned forward and squinted her eyes. "Somebody get some water and some bandages. And get the alcohol. He gonna need it."

The girls stood with their mouths agape.

Skeet yelled, "*Move!*"

Ma grabbed Pa and dragged him toward the house. Others from the village came out of their homes to help her—the Cajuns, and a few other men and women running with long white reams of bandages fluttering behind them.

Pa reached the house and tried to smile at his daughters, but only grimaced. His skin was pale.

"He say he was playin' numbers and somebody cheated him," Ma said. "Dammit, Pa! Ain't nobody got time for this right now!" She released her grip and barked orders: "Boys! Get him inside! Y'all got stuff to clean him?"

The group chasing him caught up—six men with betting slips in their hands. They yelled loudly until Ma walked out into the yard and fired the shotgun into the air to shut them up.

Still frozen to the spot, the girls turned and looked at their mother. A smoke trail curled from the muzzle of the shotgun. "If'n y'all want some..."

"He was cheatin'!" a man in a brown suit yelled.

"Who shot him?" Ma yelled. "Which one of y'all yellow bellied—"

"I shot him!" A man with dark pants and a white shirt rolled up to the elbows stepped forward and raised his fist. "Cheatin' me out my keep! Every damn week—"

Ma leveled the shotgun at him and fired. "Get *off* my land! Next time I won't miss!"

The man, now on the ground, started to yell. "You ain't miss, you bitch! Ya shot me right—"

Ma shot the man twice more. When some of the others moved toward him, she growled, "Leave that body right there!"

Skeet stepped forward, waving her cane. "You heard her! Get off this land, unless you bringin' the sheriff!"

"We goin' get that money he owe us!" one yelled.

Ma shot once more into the pack of men, her face dark with anger. The group stumbled backward. Someone yelled "Ow!" before they all turned and ran. Ma watched them until they were out of sight.

"Skeet, if that bastard get up, you keep him down!" she snapped, passing the gun to Skeet.

"Right." Skeet took the gun and motioned for the girls to go inside. "Fix your pa."

Finally, the girls moved.

Inside, they found Pa lying on the supper table. The table had been dragged away from the wall and to the middle of the floor, and the guys from the village had rested him on top of it, on his back. A few of the women working on him had blood on their skirt aprons.

"Miss, he got hit with buckshot," Louise, their neighbor and a former nurse, said. "We can't get it all out, but we can try."

Ma elbowed her way into the center of the fray. "Thanks, Louise. Do ya need anythin' else?"

"Heat the water, and put a stick in his mouth. I gotta get in there! Somebody get me a light!"

Pa groaned loud and turned his head to the side. He looked at Ma. "Sorry, baby. I ain't cheat none. That was ol' George. Always swear I owe him somethin' cuz the dummy never learn to count. Couldn't count the number of legs on a chicken without somebody drawin' him a clue."

Pee Wee laughed, but it came out more like a strangled choke. "Funny, Pa."

"Baby, I got them pralines for ya. I gave 'em to your ma. I got uh…" Pa groaned.

"Don't talk, Pa!" Ann yelled from the other side of the room. "We all is here for you!"

The men stepped away to let the girls stand next to their father while Louise worked on him. Ma gently wiped the sweat from his brow, whispering to him that everything would be okay this time.

"This time?" Betty asked.

"Ain't the first time your pa been shot," Ma answered. "Big strong man like him, this ain't nothin'. Now, kiss your pa on the forehead and wait on the porch with Skeet."

Ma spoke with such a soft, assured tone, the girls did what they were told. Each daughter kissed him and told him that they loved him. Pee Wee was last, and Betty and Ann needed to pry her off him, even though he held onto her just as tight.

"Pee Wee, you was so little when you was born…" Pa's eyes rolled up in his head.

"He was shot more than once," Louise yelled. "Get them boys. We gotta flip him."

"Girls, outside!" Ma hissed. "Now!"

They trudged outside as the men scrambled back around the table. Someone counted to three, and there was a huge noise.

They must have flipped him over, because Pa groaned loud enough to fill the house with a sound of dread and gloom.

"I'm goin' to get Teddy," Pee Wee said, bending over to tie her shoes. "She can fix him. Y'all can stay here, but I'm goin'."

Betty looked around. She remembered running into the sheriff in town, but she also knew he was the law, and he had to uphold the law, no matter what. "I gotta get the sheriff! These fools done tried to kill my pa!"

Gene peeked from around the side of the house before walking over to her. "Hey...uh...Betty. Heard your pa was shot. You okay? Ya need anythin'?" He spoke like molasses, slow and sweet. He always offered himself up to help her with anything. Anything she needed, he'd gladly get it for her. If she asked him to rip off his arm, he would.

"Gene, I need a horse. Y'all got a fast horse? I gotta get the sheriff. That man on the ground shot my pa!"

Without speaking, he grabbed her hand and pulled her along behind him, heading toward the bridge and the stables.

Pee Wee watched them go. "Wow."

"That boy got it bad," Ann said.

"I'm a go get Teddy. You comin'?"

Ann's brow furrowed. "I do want to, but I need to stay here for Ma."

Skeet yelled, "Go on! Get that hoodoo woman! Y'all ain't gonna serve no purpose round here unless you's a doctor or Jesus!"

Ann looked for Pee Wee to tell her they should head to Teddy's house, but her sister was already halfway down the trail that led to Teddy's, running at breakneck speed.

"If Pa die...I won't be able to tell him...," Ann blubbered.

"It's gonna be all right. You needs to be strong, girl. We done seen worse."

Ann wiped her eyes with the backs of her hands.

"Pee Wee gettin' outta sight!" Skeet said. "Best get to runnin'."

"Right." Ann sprinted down the path after Pee Wee. The

tears stinging her face reminded her of all the things she never got to ask Pa.

Betty and Gene rode past on two black stallions down a different trail toward town, but Ann didn't stop running, not even when she caught up to Pee Wee. They pressed on harder and ran farther.

"You all right?" Pee Wee asked, wiping the tears away.

"Dunno. There's Teddy! Over there!" Ann pointed down toward the river.

Once they stopped running, the tears stung worse.

Teddy didn't smile at them. She didn't frown either. She only stared. Then she picked up her bag, dropped whatever plant she was examining, and ran over to them.

"Somethin' happened. Is it bad?" she asked.

"I'm gonna need a bit," Pee Wee said, doubled over and leaning her butt against a large tree trunk. "My chest is burnin'. Hurts." She sat on the ground, wheezing.

Teddy looked worried and began frantically searching the bushes nearby. She grabbed a berry off the bush, tasted it, nodded, and grabbed more.

"I got a bottle of water in my sack." Teddy took it out, rinsed the berries, and gave them to Pee Wee to eat. "This'll fix that burnin'."

Teddy pressed past Ann to grab some leaves off another bush. "Watch y'self." She rubbed the leaves together and sniffed them. Then she jammed them all in her mouth and chewed for a few seconds.

Then she returned to Pee Wee, held the girl's mouth open with one hand, and placed the other on her chest. "Breathe," she said.

Then, she leaned over and blew into Pee Wee's mouth.

Pee Wee's body relaxed. The air from Teddy's mouth was cooling.

After a few more breaths, she stopped wheezing.

Teddy was still leaning over her, blowing into her mouth.

"Teddy?" Pee Wee gulped.

"Silly girl. Stay still." Teddy reached back for another handful of berries.

"What is you…"

"Eat these, then we get goin', okay?" She gave Pee Wee the berries and sat on the ground next to her.

"What's all that you did?" Ann asked.

"Hoodoo. I mean, I am 'the swamp rat.' I saves lives." Teddy spit the leaves on the ground and pointed to the plant. "That's mint. It will help her calm down and cool off. The berries'll help her breathe better. You see, hoodoo ain't all cat bones and goofer dust. Now, why y'all runnin' all back up here? Sun 'bout to set and I—"

"Pa got shot." The words fumbled from Ann's mouth. "And I think he gonna die."

The smile faded from Teddy's face. She seemed to take forever to rise to her feet. She adjusted her black head wrap and reached her hand out to Pee Wee. "Let's get goin'."

"Can ya fix him?" Ann asked. "He got shot with buck shot and somethin' in his back too."

"Mmm," Teddy said. "Let's go."

Pee Wee looked at Ann. "I feel better. Can't run all that fast, but that burnin' is gone."

"I'm a run ahead to see what's happenin'," Ann said.

"Wait. My brother done been shot plenty of times." Teddy touched a bone tied on a string around her neck. She closed her eyes for a moment. "And this is not good. All right, let's get and hope I can make it. Who shot him?"

"Some guy he was runnin' numbers with, I think." Pee Wee said.

Teddy made a small noise akin to a sigh. "All right."

The lightning bugs were out, lighting a path for them, it seemed. They followed Teddy's lanky stride down the worn trail, back to the village. She wore a white shirt, tied at the waist. It was too big for her over a pair of navy pants and heavy shoes. It felt like she cleared the path as she walked—so regal—through the waist-high bushes. The silver bangles on her left arm jingled lightly, almost creating a tune for the bugs to light themselves to.

Ann caught a whiff of Teddy. "Smell like lavender," she whispered.

"And mint." Pee Wee finally caught her breath.

Pee Wee smelled someone cooking something good. She realized she hadn't even had lunch when they went home the first time. Her stomach growled, but she kept eating the berries that Ann had gathered and seemed to have a never-ending supply of.

Ann shot a quick glance at Pee Wee. "We best hurry."

"Ann," Pee Wee whispered, "for whatever it's worth, I don't see Pa standin' around nowhere."

"Well, that's a good thing," Teddy 's voice drifted back. "And I hope you don't see him out here anytime soon."

THE SHERIFF

They heard people's voices before they reached the house. Someone barked out orders, and a few of the numbers men yelled at the house. The clopping of horses' hooves approached right behind them and then stopped at the house. They turned to see Betty and Gene dismounting.

Gene took the horses around to the side of the house.

"We tried to get the sheriff," Betty told them. "He say that he's comin' but didn't move."

"Yeah," Gene said, "he just kinda looked at us."

Betty ran over to her sisters. "Y'all okay? Pee Wee don't look so good."

"I had a hard time breathin' from runnin' so fast, is all." Pee Wee managed to say.

"Like a bat out of hell, she ran!" Ann added.

Betty looked at the two of them. "Okay, I'm gonna check on Pa."

Teddy brushed by them all and went into the house.

"Y'all got *her*?" Betty huffed. "She ain't no doctor."

"Skeet told us to get her and—" Ann stopped at the sounds of horses approaching.

The sheriff, tall and white and wearing the whitest clothing, slowly trotted his white horse down the trail toward their house. A small crowd followed behind, pointing in the direction of the girls. It looked like some of the same men as earlier.

"That's his house!" someone yelled. "You know Robert! He work on the rails and such."

The sheriff waved his hand at the group of men. "I know all about Mr. Robert Conway. If memory serves, he's been shot before. What makes this any different?" His voice seemed amused.

"Because my pa can die!" Ann yelled before she covered her mouth.

"Stupid man," Pee Wee grumbled.

"What do you girls expect with your pa runnin' numbers? There would never be no crime?" The sheriff laughed and looked around. "Seems these men want what's theirs."

Then, he walked over to the man on the ground. He pulled out a handkerchief and held it up to the man's face. He waved it over his closed eyes then made a *tsk* sound and stood up.

"Never really been to this village, but I know about your pa," he said and walked over toward the girls. "Y'all keeps to your self, huh?"

Ma stepped outside. Teddy filled the doorway behind her.

"That man shot my husband." Ma's voice was shaky. "He killed my husband. Whatcha gonna do?"

Pee Wee flopped to the ground, her eyes looking up at the sky as she mouthed the words, "He dead?"

Betty stumbled out to the porch, her cheeks blossomed bright red from crying. Ann rushed over to Pee Wee.

"We gots to have some hope, Pee Wee." Ann wrapped her arms around her little sister, "We gots to believe he gonna be okay."

"Y'all looked at him. Is he though?" Pee Wee asked as tears ran down her cheeks.

The sheriff put his handkerchief away and walked up onto the porch, toward the door. He motioned for the girls to move aside, but Teddy stepped up and blocked him. "Answer her, Earl."

"I can't right get a gauge on the situation until I see both sides, Miss Teddy. Now, if you would please..."

"Theodora."

"Excuse me." The sheriff laughed. "Miss Theodora."

"Ma'am, is that yer kin?" The sheriff pointed back to the girls. "Best get over there and comfort them. Little girls look real shook up." His tone wasn't acerbic; it was more apathetic. "Now, let me see the body."

"What is you gonna do?" Teddy, now standing close to the sheriff, seemed twice her normal size. She leaned into his face. "Remember how many times I helped you and your wife. Now, what is you gonna do?"

The sheriff leaned back, feigning shock. "Miss Theodora, are you trying to blackmail me into something?"

"I'm reminding you where we stand. Now, what is ya gonna do?"

He smirked and glanced at Ma and the men further away in the yard. "Well, nothin' happened on account of me not seein' all the evidence." He snickered, covered his mouth with the handkerchief, and stepped back down off the porch.

"We told you what happened. That man shot my husband," Ma growled. "And the whole damned mob behind him probably was in on it."

The sheriff spun on his heels to face Ma and cleared his throat. "Ya know, you're wastin' my time. I came down here and can't see the other body. This one dead in the street! Who you want me to arrest?"

Ma fumed. "I want justice. Arrest all them men."

"Why? Look like some nigger justice done took place down here." The sheriff laughed, strolled over to the dead body and kicked it. "This one shot your nigger husband, and you shot this one. Whatcha want me to do? It's one thing if them Cajuns did something, but you got niggers shootin' niggers down here. What do I care?"

Everything fell still and quiet as the sheriff walked back over to his horse, kicking up small tufts of dust. "Now unless you niggers got some serious problems, I'm gonna have to bid you good day."

The collective silence was broken by Ma cocking her shotgun and aiming it at the sheriff. "We's back on our own, huh? Never do nothin'…no-good man only help us when he need somethin'…"

Teddy pressed her hand on Ma's shoulder. "What did you want him to do?"

Ma turned and growled. "You know there's more than one. Always more than one."

Teddy's voice dropped to a whisper. "But you done killed the main one."

"I shoot this man, and that's it? Justice?" Ma kept her aim on the sheriff. "I oughta shoot one…"

"Not in front of the girls." Teddy put her hand on the barrel and lowered the shotgun. "Be better than them."

Betty, Ann, and Pee Wee stood in a small circle, Betty with her arms around both sisters. Pee Wee's face was drenched in tears. Ann's face was bright red as she tried to hold them back.

"That's it?" Betty snapped.

"That's it." Teddy stepped off the porch. "Go about your business. And you assholes, get outta town!"

The small crowd hustled together.

"Get! If I see ya in these parts, I'm a put roots on your family."

Several of the men mumbled, but they all moved off, heading for the path that led out of town. Teddy followed a short way. She stopped over the dead man and pointed.

"Come get this body!"

"No, leave it!" Ma yelled.

"Ain't gonna do no good. Bad mojo on this man anyway. He was gonna get his sooner or later." Teddy kicked at him. "Come get this body!"

Two men ran back and grabbed the legs. They left again, dragging the body behind them.

"No point in keeping that body here. Can't get nothin' from it nor do nothin' for it." Teddy walked back onto the porch. Ma walked into the house.

"That's it," Pee Wee said. "We just...that's it..."

"No! That's not it!" Ann shook her sisters off. "I say we get him. Get that asshole sheriff back and do somethin'."

"What? What is we gonna do? We got too much to do round here." Betty crossed her arms. "I loved Pa too, but I don't think he'd want us runnin' after the sheriff."

"I'm gonna get him. He ain't offer no condolence, nothin'." Ann fumbled away from her sisters and pointed at Teddy. "And Teddy didn't do nothin'! What's the point of havin' an aunt that do rootwork and she don't do nothin'?"

"Now, Patricia Ann..." Teddy started.

"No! No! They ain't gonna never respect us! Teddy, you's got power! Why ain't you gonna do nothin'? This white man let these people kill my pa! Then ain't nobody go to jail cuz Ma killed one of them?"

"What was I s'posed to do?" Teddy whispered. "He's my brother."

"He's our *pa*!" Betty said. "You coulda threw roots or somethin'! You coulda done somethin'! But you stood there lookin' stupid and ain't do nothin'! Useless." Betty ran around the house, calling for Gene.

A moment later, she'd mounted the horse and rode out front, yelling "Useless!" She pulled on the horse's reins, and it stopped trotting. "Useless!" she spat again, staring at Teddy for a spell, and then she rode on toward the bridge near the community garden.

Gene mounted the other horse and followed after her, calling her name.

Pee Wee looked up. "You shoulda done somethin', Teddy."

Ma set the shotgun down and held her arms open. "Girls! Come here, girls!"

But Pee Wee sat on the ground, Ann crossed her arms and stared.

"We goin' to make this right," Pee Wee mumbled. "I'm gonna get that sheriff."

"No, *we* gonna get that sheriff." Ann reached a hand down toward Pee Wee. "We goin' to get that sheriff and show him he can't treat us like this."

PA

Pee Wee and Ann stood in the doorway, watching them work on the body.

Pee Wee stared straight ahead at what seemed to be Pa, but maybe was nothing.

Skeet noticed her staring, guided her over to a chair, and helped her sit down. "Gonna be all right, Pee Wee," she whispered.

Pee Wee didn't speak.

The bullet had rolled out of his chest when they were working on him. All the moving, twisting, and fixing, only to hear Pa heave one huge sigh… and then to watch the bullet roll off the table and onto the floor.

Louise looked at Ma. "I'm sorry I didn't see it. If I knew… you know I woulda…"

"Louise, you did your best, and that's all I can ask." Ma walked over and put her hand on Louise's blood-covered hand. "He was probably hidin' it anyway. You know how Robert was with stuff, keepin' the best for later."

"I'm really sorry. I tried." Louise looked down at Pa's body.

"Let's get him stitched up and onto the bed. I gotta clean all this up." Ma stared at her hands. "Let me clean this up."

A few of the women at the table helped Louise finish cleaning up Robert's body. Everyone worked around Ma, who cleaned the floor with a vacant stare in her eyes. Betty walked over and helped her.

Teddy bundled some of the wraps and cotton balls they had used to work on Pa and put them in a bucket to go outside.

Then she walked Ma to her bedroom. "Let's get you cleaned up, and I'll get started on doing what I need to do."

Ma looked at Teddy. "You gonna take care of him?"

"I'll take care of everythin'. I'll do the washin' and dressin'. I have to run home and get some stuff, but I'll be right back."

Teddy closed the door behind them. Once it was shut tight, Ma wailed and cried. She sat in a chair at the foot of the bed where Pa was "resting." The window in the bedroom was wide open, allowing a slight summery breeze to sneak inside and wrap itself around Ma, like nature itself was trying to comfort her pain.

No one spoke over the sounds of Ma's mourning. The entire village was filled with quiet. It seemed as though the birds stopped chirping and the rivers stopped flowing.

Betty returned in tears, picked up the bloody towels, and threw them in a bucket. Ann moved around the room, picking things up and blindly making herself busy.

Pee Wee sat in the chair and stared off into space.

The room was silent save for the sound of scrubbing on the floor and the rinsing of towels in buckets.

Eventually, Ma's crying quieted enough for Teddy to step out of the room.

"I'm going home to get some things and change clothes. I'll take care of everything, girls." As she slid out the front door, she paused and looked back. "Pee Wee, come with me. You shouldn't be round here for all this."

Pee Wee looked up, her face devoid of emotion. "I'll be fine as long as Pa keeps standing by the door to keep them other people out."

"Whatcha mean, he standin' by the door." Teddy stepped back into the house.

"Pa, he standin' there, watchin' us. There's some folk with him: one look like a Indian lady and a brown-skin man. Big-muscled man."

"No, Pee Wee. Because if he standin' there, then he ain't in here." Teddy said, her voice shaking. "He can't be standin' over there because he gotta stay here…he can't leave us!"

"They standin' right there with Pa." Pee Wee looked just beyond Teddy and nodded her head. "Yes, okay, ma'am. I'll go."

Betty stopped, "Who you talkin' to Pee Wee?"

"She say she our grandma, and that I needs to go with Teddy."

Teddy whipped around and stared at Pee Wee, like she willed her to not see her brother standing there. Tears streamed down Teddy's cheeks and her bottom lip quivered. She stepped forward and walked to the doorway, inhaling a sweet jasmine scent that filled the room. "Smell like my ma all right. Always wore jasmine perfume."

Ann rose from the floor. She walked over and stood next to Pee Wee. "Where?"

"Over there, behind Teddy. You see?" Pee Wee raised her hand and pointed in the direction. "But they leavin' and say I gotta go with Teddy. I'm s'posed to help her get the stuff together."

"Stuff for what?" Betty asked.

"Some kinda washin'." Pee Wee trudged out the door, with Teddy following her close behind.

THE WASHING

Teddy had stopped by a few of the other cabins, gathering some fellow (but less skilled) rootworkers and people who knew Ma and Pa. A few musicians also came, carrying huge drums. Everyone was dressed in white, and the women had tied their hair up in white scarves. They all brought pots of food that filled the house with the smells of love and cooking: catfish, cornbread, stews, gumbos, and small cakes. Someone even managed to bring some pralines from the city. Women from the village scurried back and forth, finishing up the cleaning and setting the food on the table.

Pee Wee looked for Pa, and found him in the bedroom with Ma sitting next to him. He looked like he was sleeping and at peace.

She walked over to him and whispered, "Everythin' gonna be okay, Pa. We got some of the other ladies here. They gonna help clean you up real nice." She laid a small hand on Pa's forehead, bent down, and kissed him.

Ma sat close to Pa, resting her hands on his. Her eyes were bloodshot. She forced herself to smile at Pee Wee through the tears.

"It's okay, Ma. It's okay." Pee Wee whispered. "Pa is here watchin' over us. It's gonna be fine."

"Come get a plate," Teddy whispered, peeking in from the door.

Ma groaned as she got up slowly and walked toward the door, shoulders drooping. "Be sure the girls eat."

"I told you, I will take care a everythin.'"

Ma patted the back of Teddy's hands and made her way to the table. Pee Wee followed them out.

"Looks so good," Ma said as she took a chair. "Thanks, y'all."

Teddy watched the girls move around the room by necessity and not desire. No one wanted to eat, but they needed to eat.

The sun was starting to set outside when she went into the bedroom and sat on a chair next to her brother's body.

Betty quietly followed her to the doorway and stood, watching.

"Robert, I can't even believe you done somethin' so stupid and left them girls and they ma." Teddy shook her head, resting it in her hands. "But I'm gonna make sure you get to the ancestors. It's the least I can do, Robert. And I promise to teach the girls the old ways, so we don't lose any of this tradition. This here is ours, and we gotta keep it for ourselves. Use it on the people."

"What you gonna teach us?" Betty asked. "How to do what? I mean, you ain't done nothin' to the sheriff."

"I'm teachin' you the old ways of how to take care of your pa to ensure he get to his ancestors. These things you should know." Teddy's tone was sharp but not commanding. "One day, you gonna need someone to do this to you, if'n you want to see us all again."

"Shoulda taught that sheriff somethin' first," Betty snapped.

"And let y'all sit and suffer? Why? You tryin' to tell me that white man is more important than your pa? I'm not sure your pa would see it that way. If'n ya want, I'll go take care of him now. But lemme tell you somethin'..." Teddy looked up at Betty and straight into her eyes. "Rootwork take time. You best bet, no matter what you believe, he goin' to get his."

Betty met Teddy's steel gaze with one of her own. "You sure?"

"I promise on my life."

Resigned, Betty walked into the room and joined her. "What I gotta do?"

Teddy started talking and moving around the room. She took an empty bucket from the corner and set it close to her bags. "Set up candles everywhere and light 'em all, and then grab another bucket—that bucket of water I put out near the fire outside. First, we gotta do the foot washin'."

Betty rushed out of the room and returned with the bucket.

She watched as Teddy opened one of the bags she'd brought with her and began pulling out small jars filled with brilliant-colored herbs and flowers, a mortar and pestle, a metal bowl, and several small wrapped burlap bags of spices. She set them all up on the chair where she had sat a moment ago. Next, she began mixing herbs in a metal bowl.

"Get your sisters. There's more power in three than just me."

"What?"

"Three, like the Father, the Son, and the Holy Spirit. It's three of y'all girls. Strength in threes." Teddy made a motion with her hand, ushering Betty out the room.

Betty returned, literally dragging Pee Wee into the room. Ann followed them.

"Pee Wee and Ann, take your pa's shoes off while I fix this." Teddy dipped her hand into the metal bowl and swirled the ingredients around. "Frankincense, myrrh, camphor, flower, hyssop, and some prayed-over water."

"What's all this?" Ann asked.

"To help. Now get them shoes off."

They looked at Pa's body laid out on the bed. He looked like he was asleep. They hadn't realized how big of a man he was until they'd seen him like this, lying under a white sheet with his shoes on.

Pee Wee and Ann worked fast, untying his shoes and dropping them to the floor. Teddy prayed over the water.

She paused and looked at the girls. "Y'all know how to tie a wrap on your head?"

"Yeah?" Betty responded. "Why?"

"Gotta tie the wraps over all your head, cover all the hair. All-white wraps. I left them on the chair over there. Tuck all your hairs underneath, anything hanging will have to be cut and burned. It's all gotta be covered."

"That's why you all dressed in white?" Betty asked.

Pee Wee walked over and picked up the white pieces of fabric for their hair. She gave one to Betty and another to Ann, saving the last for herself. She held up larger swaths of white fabric that the girls used to wrap around themselves, with Teddy securing each one. Once their clothing was all covered by the white fabric, they just needed to put the scarves on their heads.

"Yes. And outta respect for the dead. You need to understand that your pa is takin' a journey. He goin' home, and we gotta wash all this earth from his feet to make the journey easier for him. He's leaving behind the trappings of this place and going somewhere else clean. Stepping into the realm of our kin a clean and new man."

Teddy tied a wrap on Pee Wee's head and tucked her hairs in.

"Let me see you." She stepped back and looked at the girls. "Good, he'd be so proud. Now, let's get started."

Teddy passed each of them a white towel, and they moved the chair and the metal bowl over to his feet. She showed them how to raise the towel over the feet and let the water fall down onto it. "The feet can't be lowered. They have to stay up."

Pee Wee passed the bowl to Teddy, and Betty took a white towel to dry each foot.

Pee Wee stepped out of the way until Teddy took the bowl. She set it in a corner of the room before she walked over and took the girls' hands. "Put your hands on his feet. We goin' to have words and pray."

Ma popped into the doorway. She didn't speak but walked over and joined them. Soon, she was leading the prayer as they swayed in silence.

"Now, we anoint with the oil and put these here white socks on him."

"What's in the oil?" Ann asked as she passed the brown bottle to Ma.

"Ash, eggshells, castor oil, and other stuff. Don't worry, Pa won't have stank feet." Teddy joked.

When Ma finished anointing his feet with the oil, Ann and Pee Wee slipped a white sock over each of his feet.

"Now, go wash hands. We gotta wash his head and hair." Teddy picked up the other bucket and mixed more herbs and oil into it with the blessed water.

Ma grabbed one of the white head wraps off the back of the chair. She whispered to Teddy, "I forgot this. I just wanted…I just…" Ma's shoulders folded forward as her body shook with tears. She dropped the head wrap on the floor.

"I'm sure he won't mind. He'll understand." Teddy's fingers danced as they smoothed the wrap down and pushed Ma's hair beneath it.

Ma composed herself and walked to the other side of the bed and ran her fingers through Pa's wavy black hair.

Betty, Ann, and Pee Wee stood behind her, giving her some time with Pa during the ceremony.

"You gotta run the water through the hair," Teddy said. "Put a bucket underneath and save that water for me. While you do it, pray for your pa. Pray for him to be blessed and allowed to go to his ancestors."

They followed her instructions. Ma was the last one to run oil through his hair and part it. She combed it over and parted it with her fingers. A few of her tears fell on his forehead while she did it. Teddy reached over, with a clean white towel, and wiped them off.

When they were done, Teddy called as many of the people from the village into the room as could fit. Then she began: "'Yea, though I walk through the valley of death...'"

🍃 PEE WEE

They been down there cookin' and dancin' and playin' music for days. Days since my pa was put in the ground at that place by Teddy's house. Days since that white sheriff ain't do nothin'. Days of food and music. Teddy said somethin' about "Africa take him home." She used another word: -*voke* somethin'...*invoke*? She say, "Spirits invoke him something..." I stopped listenin'. They call the spirits up and take him away, then they tell the spirits to go away. Don't make no sense.

Ann bring me food and Ma come check on me, but I feel like the whole world is layin' on me and I can't move. I wanna cry, but I can't make no tears. I wanna go do somethin' and be mad, but where I gonna go? I'm Pee Wee. Nobody take me serious.

I been thinkin' though. I saw a blow-spell in one of them pages of Teddy's hoodoo book. I don't know all the words, but it's a spell that ya blow in someone face and they can't move on account of the par—parly—not movin'. At least, that's what Ann said the word meant.

"Pee Wee, you comin' down today?" Ann set a really good smellin' plate of food next to my bed. "We all worried 'bout you."

I turned away. "Not today."

She started to walk down the stairs.

"Ann, what's that word for when you can't move, that I asked you?"

"Paralyze. Why?"

"Just curious." I say it to myself. "*Paralyze.*"

"Pee Wee, don't do nothin' stupid." Ann stopped on the steps. "At least, not by yourself."

"Yep."

She kept walking down the stairs.

Paralyze. I'm gonna get that sheriff. He can't come here and call us names, and arrest nobody for killing my pa. And I'm so tired.

I ate the food Ann brought up and fell asleep again. When I woke up, Ma was sittin' on the edge of the bed. "Pee Wee, you stink. You gotta bathe at least."

"Ma, I don't wanna do nothin'. Everythin' hurt. Like my heart hurt, and my head, and it even hurt to look sometimes."

"Pee Wee, look at me."

I turn over and see Ma. She look older. Like she been cryin' for days. "Your pa was such a smooth-talkin' man. He rode up to my house on this horse, lookin' like he was important, and asked my pa if he could take me out. Your pa was a good man. He wouldn't want you to stay in bed all day, mopin' and bein' sad."

"Ma, they play music for days outside. Days… It's not happy times."

For once, I don't got much to say.

"It's a time for us to remember all the good things in your pa's life. Like you and your sisters, how he was so proud of y'all. Specially you, Pee Wee. He was your age when he started workin' on the railroad. Never learned to read or write. He just used his big hand and wrote a small X to make his mark." Ma laughed. "Big ol' hand and makin' this lil X on stuff. Pa was funny. He asked me if he should try to sign a mark or his name on all the birth certificates for y'all. So, he learned to write his name. He was proud on them days, sayin', 'When I die, my girls will see my name on them certificates, and it'll make them proud to know that they pa wrote it.'"

I sat up and looked at Ma. Hunched over, sad, Ma with the pretty curls in her hair. Ma digging her fists into her eyes and glancing at me. She smile real pretty.

"I'm comin' down, Ma. I just...the sheriff."

"He done what he was s'pose to do. Them boys ain't come back, so no problems. I got an eye for an eye, and that's it." Ma wiped her hands like she cleaned them. "It's all done."

"Eye for an eye, just like the Bible?"

Ma nodded. "Just like the Bible."

"And nobody gonna do nothin'."

"What's to do?"

I felt a little better until the next morning. Then, I got up and went downstairs, because I couldn't breathe no more upstairs. 'Sides, I hear a bunch of noise outside.

Looked like fog had settled to the ground, and it was barely light out. Barely. Even the stars was out when I looked up.

"What happen?" I see folks in nightgowns running with buckets of water, and a fire off in them woods where that old voodoo lady house was. I see my sisters and Teddy runnin' and hear the horses comin' up behind me.

"He always turn up like a bad penny," I hear someone whisper. "That man is bad luck."

A lady gave me a bucket filled with water and told me to follow. Ain't have time to even think, just run.

The sheriff got off the horse and walked toward the fire. He put his hands on his hips, like he all high an mighty, and say, "Boy! Y'all niggers have some bad luck. Maybe y'all ought to move or somethin'. Give this land to me. I'll buy it off ya…"

"Ain't for sale, Sheriff!" a man yelled.

I threw the bucket of water on the fire, but I was so angry seein' that man just standin' there, jokin'. If I had powers like Teddy, I'd do somethin'. Or I woulda done did somethin'.

"Well, look at you. You wanna leave here and come work for me? On account of y'all lil village is burnin'." The sheriff sound like he was singing to me. He grabbed my chin and held my head up. "You look like a hard worker."

Everything in me started burnin'. My face was hot. I wanted to punch him. I wanted to hit him for actin' like we ain't even have nothin' happen. My pa is gone!

"You gots to leave," I said.

"Oh, I gots to leave?" the sheriff mocked. "And where you sleepin' tonight, gal? Keep it up and the rest a your village will burn down too."

"I'm a get you. I'm a get you for what you did," I said so low I didn't know he heard me.

"What I do? Let your nigger pappy die? He owed all of us money. No big loss. You're a youngin' and can find another pappy. Your ma, she not old. Still sturdy. Wouldn't mind if y'all worked for my wife. She can use help with them girls."

What girls? I thought.

He laughed. "*I* could be your pappy."

Teddy say when someone walk on your grave, you get a shiver up your back. I felt all my bones in my spine get scared when he said that.

"I got a pa. Better'n you and them girls."

"Them's the girls I helped his wife have on account of her not bein' able to have no children." Teddy walked up behind me. "You just gonna let this burn? Not gonna get the fire brigade?"

"Looks like the fire put itself out." He stepped closer to Teddy. "Not unless there's a lil spark left for me to work with."

I ain't dumb and I ain't all that smart, but what is happening? He speak to Teddy not like he kinda scared of her, like he want somethin'.

Teddy stepped in his face. "Don't come back round here. You done enough."

"Gotta check on my people in the parish, y'know?"

"We fine on our own, Earl. Leave and don't come back."

He stared at Teddy, then at me. He tipped his hat and smiled. "I knows where ya live Teddy. Lets say I pay ya a visit there." He walked to his horse and mounted it. "I may need somethin' from ya soon."

He laughed and rode down the path as the sun came up.

The voodoo house was burned. Wasn't nothin' there but some part of the frame and a stone fireplace.

Betty walked over from the fire and sat on the porch. She looked tired.

Ann sat too. She had a bucket and looked even more tired.

"Where's Ma?" I asked.

"Pee Wee. You finally got outta bed. Great day in the mornin'!" Ann smiled, despite her face being covered with dirt. "Don't worry bout that voodoo house. That's the only one they got."

"Somebody did this?" I asked.

"We all know it was the sheriff. We don't bother nobody, and he still think we botherin' someone. If not, he come botherin' us...take our girls, scare our men, make us pay money for protection, and we ain't protected. I'm just ready to pack up and leave."

"None of this is fair. We ain't even do nothin'." I sat next to them. "I'm gonna get that sheriff."

"Your name is Pee Wee," Ann growled. "Whatcha gonna do? You's not knee high to a fly."

I think she makin' a joke on me, but she look powerful mad.

"When we was at Teddy's, I read some papers. I'm gonna get that man. I'm gonna make him apologize to us and Ma."

"It's not enough for him to apologize," Teddy said, stepping up behind us. "Don't worry, girls, he'll pay. What go round, come round."

"Whatcha gonna do? Hoodoo him to death?" Betty snapped. "Eat all these black cats and drink this pee?"

Betty was back to bein' mad at Teddy, on account of nothin'. Teddy ain't kill Pa. That other man did, and he gone. They shot my Pa, and ain't nobody do nothin'.

"If she say, she gonna do," Ma said.

Betty stomped off somewhere, sayin' stuff under her breath.

I clapped my hands, because Teddy was gonna do somethin'. She didn't look happy or sad; she just looked serious. And I know that's gotta be big.

I gotta do somethin' with them rootwork spells I saw in that book. Anything.

Somebody waved to me by the voodoo house, in the smoke. While everybody talkin', I sneak over there and don't see no one but a lot of smoke.

"S'pose ya lookin' for somethin'?" The voice was behind me, then all around me.

"Who that?" I smelled some sweet smoke, not the fire smoke, but like tobacco.

"I'll tell ya how to do some stuff, if'n ya got somethin' to give." The voice sound like an ol' lady, like she whisperin' or somethin'.

"Where you at?" I look around but don't see nothin'.

"Pee Wee! Dammit!" Ann made me jump when she ran up on me. "Come on back home! Somebody said they saw you over here! What you doin' anyway?"

"I thought I saw somethin', maybe heard somethin'..." I tried to look around.

"Ain't nobody over here, unless...you seein' spirits or somethin'." Ann looked around. "Did ya see her? The voodoo lady?"

"I mean, I ain't *see* nobody. I said I heard somethin'. You done probably scared her off anyway." I started to walk back home when I saw her, off in the woods.

She was a hunchbacked-lookin' thing with a pipe. She had a white wrap around her head and a white dress on. And she was smokin' the pipe, like all the folks do. Only she had some white paint on her face too. She smiled at me, and I wasn't scared. I wanted to walk over but Ann was tryin' to pull me back.

All my life people pullin' or pushin' on me.

"What you see?" Ann whispered in my ear. "See somethin'?"

"Um, no. I thought I did, but I ain't see nothin'." I followed Ann back home.

One day, I'm gonna push back, and y'all should be scared.

A VISIT

Ashort time after the funeral, Ma sent Ann and Pee Wee to Teddy's house for Pee Wee to get out the house and do something "aside from mopin' around all damned day."

As they walked the path to Teddy's house, Pee Wee jumped around, excited, asking Ann what she thought Teddy was gonna do to the sheriff. "I hope she make him into a cat!"

Ann stopped and slapped her forehead. "You's can't make him into no cat."

"Why not? It's rootwork." Pee Wee jumped in front of Ann and bounced on tiptoe, blocking her path.

"Rootwork kinda helps things along, but it can't change you. Like, I can make a fella like me, but I can't make his rooster into a man if'n he don't wanna like me."

Pee Wee stopped walking and picked at a green plant. She sniffed it, then popped it into her mouth. "Mint. Make your breath smell better and your mouth a little cold."

"You sure is learnin' from Teddy, Pee Wee. I know wouldn't pick up nothin' off the ground and eat it unless it was cleaned. God knows, somethin' coulda peed on that leaf." Ann leaned over and looked at the plant. "I think I even see some scat around it."

"No, Teddy showed me how to read the green. Ain't no scat, just you messin'." Pee Wee pushed past her.

Ann ran up behind her. "You ever notice Teddy always spot us in the woods and gotta take us to her place?"

Pee Wee pulled leaves from a different bush and tossed them at Ann. "So?"

"Just thinkin'." Ann followed, brushing the leaves from her clothes. "Anyway, Betty say she leavin' us next month. She really goin' to do it."

"Who leavin'? Teddy?"

"No, Betty! She mad, and she leavin'."

Pee Wee stopped jumping around. "Mad about what? And how you know?"

"She told me. She goin' to that finishin' school. She asked me to go with her, but I don't wanna. I wanna stay with Teddy and get real good at rootwork."

Pee Wee's shoulders slumped forward. "I don't like that."

"Well, Ma say we gotta do what we gonna do like Pa was here. She done put down good money for Betty to go. Whatcha wanna do for school?"

They walked along in silence. Birds whistled above them, and the smell of wet earth filled their nostrils as they glanced at the river, frothing and crashing over rocks near the shore. Spanish moss slithered around tree trunks, reaching for them as they strolled.

When they reached the cemetery where Pa was buried, Pee Wee grabbed a handful of flowers and went inside. She sat on a rock she'd placed at Pa's feet and spoke to him.

"Pa, whatcha think I should do? Study with Teddy or go back to school?"

"You still like talkin' to Pa?" Ann said, sitting next to her. "Can't ya see him?"

"I looked." Pee Wee arranged the flowers over the dirt. "Sometimes he stay real far back. He don't get too close. Mouth look weird, like he can't talk."

"Teddy probably sewed his lips together to keep him from tellin' us secrets." Ann laughed, until Pee Wee stared at her.

"You think...you really think..."

"I dunno. I was just jokin' but..."

Pee Wee pointed to some far-off woods. "He over there. Let's go."

Pee Wee snickered. "I know cuz I can see it's him."

"You can see everybody, Pee Wee. All them dead folks. How you know they not jokin' with you?" Ann reached forward to stop Pee Wee from leaving.

"Because that's Pa. He won't tease us like that." Pee Wee pulled away from her and took off running toward the woods.

Ann followed her, stumbling over rocks and trying to avoid fresh clumps of dirt. The cemetery was half-rundown and one wrong step could mean a broken leg or something.

Pee Wee stopped at a clearing and faced a rock. She crossed her arms and spoke to someone, "...and then Ann said it wasn't you, and I was like, yeah it is." Pee Wee stepped back and nodded. "Everybody sad, but we's gettin' along as best we can, Pa."

"Psst! Is he on that rock?" Ann asked. "Is you sure it's him?"

"Whatcha think? I'm just talkin' to myself?" Pee Wee looked toward the rock. "He say you need to stop givin' me a hard time."

"Really? What else?"

"He said you gotta give me your cornbread at the next meal cuz it'll make him happy. And next time they bring pralines, you gotta gimme them too..."

"I don't think Pa's on that rock, knucklehead." Ann swiped a clawed hand in front of Pee Wee.

"I think you just hit Pa."

"Tell him to hit me back." Ann put her hands on her hips and smirked. "Matter of fact, tell him that I won't give you my cornbread, you gonna gimme your fish and—"

A rustling close by startled them. Ann jumped in front of Pee Wee, who pulled Ann back away from the sound. When they both looked at the spot of shrubs and trees where they heard sound coming from and saw Teddy stepping from behind some trees, they sighed.

"Y'all look like a chicken 'bout to be cut up and fried!" Teddy laughed. "What y'all doin' over here?" She wore a black hat with a huge brim to block out the sun, all-black overalls, a long-sleeve blue shirt, and heavy boots.

"We was on our way to you."

"That's good to hear. What for?"

"Do stuff…" Ann said. "Ma told me to take Pee Wee out."

Teddy leaned back and rubbed her chin. "Well, c'mon then. I got somethin' for y'all to see."

"Is it the sheriff? He dead yet?" Pee Wee spurted.

Ann shot a stare at Pee Wee. "Shut up! I told you 'bout that!"

"Told her 'bout what?" Teddy led them through the high grass and back through the cemetery. She stopped at her brother's grave, fixed the flowers, and set a candle on it.

"What's that for?" Pee Wee asked.

Teddy struck a match and lit the wick. "Show him where to go if he lost." She straightened up and blew out the match. "Now, what I don't need is you worryin' 'bout that sheriff. He ain't none of your problem."

"Why not? He told me he want me to work for his wife!" Pee Wee yelled.

Ann shook her head. "He did not."

"Yeah! He did!" Pee Wee whipped around and stared at Ann and Teddy. "He say he can be my pa! My pa!"

Ann sucked air in and covered her mouth.

Teddy's jaw clenched. "He say what?"

"He say he can be my pa! You gotta do somethin', Teddy!"

Teddy's body stiffened before she closed her eyes and exhaled. "Why you think I ain't already done somethin'?"

"What! What you do?" Pee Wee's anger turned to excitement.

"Let's get to my place. I got somethin' to show ya." Teddy started walking.

"Is it the sheriff's dead body?" Pee Wee asked eagerly.

Teddy laughed and wouldn't say. "What y'all doin' over there anyway?"

"Pee Wee say she was talkin' to Pa. I don't believe her. I mean, Pa told her that I needed to give her my cornbread and stuff."

Teddy smirked. "Really? Why would my brother tell you that?"

Pee Wee raised her shoulders and smiled. "Cuz I's a growin' girl?"

"Did ya believe her?" Teddy asked Ann.

"At first, yeah. But when she was askin' for my cornbread, I know that wasn't Pa. He want me to always eat my cornbread. If'n he said give up your beans, I know it's him."

"Why?" Teddy chuckled and kept walking.

"Because Pa always ate all my beans, so Ma wouldn't get mad."

TEDDY'S WORD

Pee Wee ran the entire distance to Teddy's house and climbed the ladder ahead of the other two. She fluttered around the house, opening cabinets and pulling up the sheets on the bed.

"I ain't think you could hide a body in here," she said. "Where he at?"

Ann arrived, breathless, and sat on the bed. "What done got into you? I done lost my breath tryin' to keep up."

Teddy walked in behind her and gave Ann some herbs. "Chew this. I gave it to your sister before. It'll calm ya down."

"Smell like peppermint."

"It ain't. Just chew it." Teddy walked over and grabbed Pee Wee by the shoulders. "Have a seat and some herbs too, Pee Wee."

"What for?" Pee Wee asked.

"To calm down." Teddy said.

Did ya kill him? I hope ya did." Pee Wee sat in a chair next to the bed.

Teddy floated around the room, pulling papers together. "I want y'all to know that all that work we done over the summer—all the writin' and stuff—I got it bound together."

She held up several pieces of paper sewn together. They looked like very thick pamphlets.

"What is this?" Pee Wee asked.

"It's an end to all this."

"But what is it?" Ann reached out and took the papers.

"Gonna be a book." Teddy smiled.

Pee Wee furrowed her eyebrows and took a few pamphlets. "You said surprise. I thought you meant about pa."

"This here just paper." Ann fanned the papers in the air. "Books need a cover, right?"

Pee Wee and Ann looked at each other, then at Teddy.

"What's so special 'bout a book?" Ann asked.

"When you die, you gotta die with all of you, else you don't really get no peace. You don't give nobody peace neither, 'til that one part a you is back in you. Understand?"

Ann thumbed through the papers and glanced at Pee Wee. "Nope."

Someone knocked at the door, silencing everyone.

Teddy smiled. "Right on time."

Their eyes followed her out of the room.

A hushed whispering drifted in from the enclosed porch. When Teddy stepped back inside, she motioned for the girls to join her.

A familiar man stood on the porch. He smiled and bowed. "Bonjour, ladies."

"Who this?" Ann asked.

"Wait." Pee Wee stepped closer to the man to look at his face before she pressed the man aside. She looked out the screened-in porch, down toward the water. "He didn't come with ya, did he?" she asked the man.

"You tell me, chéri." Beaux smiled and turned to Ann. "She remember me. Surprised you don't."

"It's Beaux. That guy we saw a buncha weeks ago. The one with Isaac. Little boy." Pee Wee glanced around outside the house. "Isaac ain't come with ya?"

"Well, he did leave. Remember?"

"I was just hopin'…y'know." Pee Wee whipped around. "Why you here?"

"Teddy asked me for a favor. I am ready. We just have to get what I need." He reached out and took the pamphlets from Ann. "I need this first."

"Oh." Ann hiccuped.

"When do we go?" Teddy reached around the doorway and grabbed a small black silk bag.

"When you ready."

"This is the rest that I owe ya." She slipped the bag into his hands and clasped hers around them. "Please. It's the least I can—"

"You done more for me than I can ever ask. Consider this a favor." He pushed the bag back toward Teddy.

Pee Wee reached out. "If'n y'all don't wanna keep it, I can keep what ever it is."

"Now, now. Calm down, Pee Wee." Teddy took the bag. "And we can thank Beaux for comin' by. We will be out to your place soon. Everythin' else ready?"

"We have more people than you think," he said. "A lot of people don't like that man. *Demain.* Sunset."

"I have to check. Maybe a blood moon tomorrow." Teddy's eyes sparkled and she tried to stifle a laugh, but the smile on Beaux's face made her laugh anyway. "This is better. We can come on out tomorrow."

"Blood moon makes it better," Beaux said and smiled. He and Teddy laughed, "Don't forget all the—"

"We all been waitin' a long time for this. He had this comin' to him for awhile." Teddy grinned.

Pee Wee and Ann looked at each other and shrugged.

"What's goin' on tomorrow?" Pee Wee asked.

"Miss Teddy, the pleasure is mine. Can't wait." Beaux made an elaborate presentation of bowing and kissing Teddy's hand.

Teddy and Beaux cackled before he waved and climbed down the ladder.

"What is wrong with them?" Pee Wee mumbled, loud enough only for Ann to hear.

"What the hell is a blood moon?" Ann asked.

"Makes all things better. Specially what we got planned for tomorrow." Teddy ushered the girls back inside. "Listen, tomorrow I'm goin' to see Beaux, and I want all three of y'all to come. Maybe your ma too."

"Why? What we gonna tell her?"

"Tell her that I said that 'it's gonna happen.' That's all ya gotta say. Tell her the whole town can't come but a few folks can." She laughed. "We's gonna have us a good time!"

Pee Wee lay in bed, listening to the crickets outside the window. Someone played a fiddle in the distance. Low tones from conversations drifted in through the window like secrets escaping peoples' lips. Outside the window, the round, white moon cast beams down onto the leaves across the way. Shadows moved through the burned remains of the former voodoo house like ghosts. She tossed and turned until she kicked the sheets off and went downstairs in her white dress pajamas.

Ma sat in a chair in the corner of the room with a huge bowl, stirring.

"Whatcha makin'?" Pee Wee asked, pulling a stool up at her feet.

"Cornbread for tomorrow. Do me a favor: get that skillet off the shelf and grease it for me."

Pee Wee grabbed the heavy iron skillet off the shelf, walked over to the stove, and grabbed a jar of lard. She pulled the dishrag off the front of the stove, dipped it into the lard, and rubbed it over the inside of the skillet.

"You know what's gonna happen tomorrow?" Pee Wee asked as she wiped.

Ma laughed to herself. "Everything gonna be right with the world is what's gonna happen."

"I don't understand." She finished and wrapped the rag around the handle on the skillet. "It's ready."

Ma lumbered over and poured the cornbread batter into the skillet. She smiled to herself. "Betty is gonna leave, you know."

"Okay."

"And we leavin' too."

"What?" Pee Wee's hands shook. "Why?"

"It's time, baby. After all this, I got in touch with my kin, and we got some land in Arkansas." Ma grunted and put the skillet in the oven. "This place hold nothin' but bad for me now. And Betty leavin', well, I gotta worry 'bout you and Ann. But I can't stay here no longer. It's like your pa is here and he all around me, but I can't touch him."

"That's why we should stay!" Pee Wee yelled. "I don't wanna go!"

"I don't know what to tell ya. School start in 'bout a month or so, gotta get you situated and stuff." Ma groaned as she walked back over to the chair.

Pee Wee snatched the empty cornbread bowl off the stove and dumped water into it. She picked it up and walked out the back door to wash it. She vibrated with rage. She didn't want to leave. All she had was this place, all her memories of her pa were here.

She looked up from washing the bowl and saw Betty walking toward her, holding Gene's hand, laughing.

"Pee Wee! You look lower than a bow-legged toad." Betty sat next to her on the step. "What's goin' on?"

Pee Wee opened her mouth to speak but a sob poured out before she could stop it. Betty looked at Gene and motioned for him to leave. Pee Wee's hands shook. She almost dropped the bowl. Her body shivered as tears ran down her cheeks.

"Come on, give me that." Betty took the bowl from Pee Wee.

"You don't understand! Nobody understand me!" Pee Wee stood. Her white dress pajamas swung in a light breeze. "Nobody listen! What 'bout what I want!!"

Betty set the bowl on the step and stood. "Pee Wee?"

"You leavin', Ma leavin', Ann leavin', and me, I'm leavin'. I don't wanna go! Can't I go to finishin' school or somethin' with you?"

"I think Ma already paid for it. She been payin' for awhile."
Betty reached out to touch Pee Wee. "But I'm sure we can talk
to—"

"Ain't nothin' to talk 'bout!" she yelled. "Everybody done
made plans for Pee Wee! Pushin' and pullin' at me, and I never
ever get to say nothin'. Like everybody know what's best for me
but me!"

"You just a kid!" Betty snapped. "You need someone to look
after ya!"

"Not like you care! You ain't even goin' to be here!"

Ma stood in the doorway. "Pee Wee! Hattie! You don't
disrespect your sister like that!"

"All y'all pushin'…all y'all pullin'…what if I did a spell and
made y'all disappear! Huh? I been practicing some! I know
what I'm doin'! I make this whole place gone, then what!
Nobody yell at me no mo'!" Pee Wee rammed her fist into her
eyes, trying to stop the tears.

"You don't—" Ann started.

"What? I don't what, Ann?" Pee Wee yelled.

"We's just tryin' to look out for ya—" Betty started, but Ma
raised her hand to silence her.

Pee Wee glared at all of them then whirled and ran, barefoot,
across the village. She ran until her legs turned her toward the
bridge that connected their cabins to the horse stables. She ran
across the bridge, releasing a scream that had pent up inside
her since her pa died. She ran and screamed until her legs
shook and her voice was gone.

When she finished, she sat on the ground near the stables,
cheeks wet with tears, and screamed again. She rubbed her fists
into her eyes and doubled over. She didn't remember falling
asleep, but she had strange dreams of someone picking her up
from the ground and carrying her.

When she woke up, the morning sunlight blinding her, she
discovered she was in a strange room, in an unfamiliar bed.
And there was a stranger sitting beside her, watching over her.

"You want some water?" he asked softly.

She jumped up and looked around. "Who is you? They send you to get me? Because I'm not goin' back! I'm sick of 'em all!!"

"Who?" The man's skin was the same color as henna. His jet-black hair was parted down the middle and in two braids. He wore a brown shirt and tan pants. He moved slowly toward her with a cup of water.

"All them folk on the other side of the bridge." Pee Wee wiped at her face with the back of her hand. "My home. They send you cause I'm too small or somethin'?"

"I am a friend of Theodora." He smiled. "Besides, you ran over here. This is where I live. I haven't seen anyone but a lonely girl crying for her pa in her sleep."

"Me, huh?"

"Yes."

"You say you know Teddy?"

"Yes."

"Where am I?" She took the water and gulped it down.

"By the stables. You ran across the bridge screaming last night." He took the cup and set a plate of grits on the bed in front of her. "Please eat. I understand you're going on a big trip soon."

"How you know?" Pee Wee picked up the plate and started to scoop the grits into her mouth with the spoon. "Ain't no sugar on the grits. You got sugar?"

With a gentle smile, he gave her a small white cup. She sprinkled the sugar on the grits and kept eating.

"You seem very hungry."

"How you know 'bout my trip?" Pee Wee's mouth was full of grits when Teddy stepped into the doorway.

"We gotta getcha home, Pee Wee," she said.

"But how he know 'bout my trip?"

Teddy grinned. "Ask him."

"I saw you leave in a dream." His low voice filled the room. "You are going to make a big decision, little lady."

"Where I'm goin'?" Pee Wee passed the plate back to him. "And what's your name?"

"I am the one they call 'Lone Wolf' in your tongue. My mother was a seer, and I am too." He walked over to a bucket and placed the plate inside it. "Do you need more water?"

"No, I guess…I guess…yeah." Pee Wee peered around the room. "You live here and take care of the horses?"

"You can say that."

"Talkin' to you is like talkin' to a Sunday school teacher, I can't never get a straight answer." Pee Wee sipped at the water.

"I've got a jacket for you." Teddy held a black jacket out to her. "Still got on your nightclothes."

Pee Wee looked down and sighed.

"I take care of the horses and help with the garden." He glanced at Teddy. "I visit Theodora sometimes. She visits me."

"Oh, he your boyfriend? Cuz Ann was wonderin' why you ain't have no man round your house." Pee Wee blurted. "I mean, don't make me no difference."

"I don't need a man to be independent, Pee Wee," Teddy said. "I don't need a man for anything I can do myself. You need to learn that too."

"Tell Betty then. She all over Gene last night, lookin' like a snake 'bout to strangle him." Pee Wee gave Lone Wolf his cup. "Thanks Mister Wolf, sir. I appreciate it."

He nodded his head.

"I ain't even know you folks ate grits! I thought y'all ate corn and fish."

"The world is much bigger than here, little lady. We eat all types of things. And I do like sugar in my grits too."

"Oh," Pee Wee felt her cheeks redden, "Sorry, Mister Wolf sir.

Lone Wolf smiled at her. "Pee Wee, it's okay. Remember what I told you." He nodded at Teddy, who scooped Pee Wee up off the bed.

But Pee Wee jumped out of her arms. "Can I stay with ya, Mister Wolf? I ain't no trouble. I's small, and I'm a real hard worker. I don't wanna go on no trip. I don't even wanna go back home."

"I would be honored if you stayed, but the world has other plans for you. Your journey starts from home, not from here."

"What happened to your pa?" Lone Wolf asked.

"He got killed, and nobody wanna do nothin'. Sheriff come round and say stuff to us, like he wanna take us away and stuff. I know about that gal. The slave one that worked for the white lady—named LaLaurie or somethin' like it—and her ma set the kitchen on fire. I know how the gal ran up and jumped off'n the house cuz she don't wanna work for no white woman that beat her. I know a lot."

Lone Wolf raised his eyebrows. "Really?"

"Yup! And if I gotta jump off this bridge and be brave like her, then I'll do it. I'm not movin', and I'm not goin' back!" Pee Wee braced herself in the doorway.

Teddy sat on the bed. "So, what are you gonna do?"

"Whatcha mean?"

Teddy crossed one leg over the other. "Say Lone Wolf lets you stay here, help with the horses, what are you gonna do?"

"I'll work hard and make money. Then, I'll go to school and...and..."

"I don't get paid much to work on the horses, Pee Wee. I get to live here free and take from the garden. Once in a while, I may see a few distant members of my family, but this is all I do. Taking care of animals is something that's very meaningful to me."

"Oh, so you can't read or somethin'?"

"I can read and write, but I want you to know that this is what makes me happy. This is my purpose." He spoke slowly to her. "I do this because it is something I love to do. It makes me happy. What makes you happy? Not finishing school and living with an Indian? Eating fruits and vegetables and stinking of animals all day?"

"I don't think you stink, Mister." Pee Wee kicked at the dirt.

"Will this make you happy? You won't see the world. You won't learn anything else. You'll just be here, all day, all the time, moving this and cleaning that. Do you understand, Pee Wee?"

Pee Wee sighed.

"How old are you?" Lone Wolf asked.

"I am ten and a half, almost eleven." She stuck her chest out.

"Seems like ten is really a big number, yes?"

"Ten is huge; it's almost twenty!" Pee Wee grinned. "But you can't get me to change my mind, Mister Wolf. I'm still not goin' back home. I'll go where I can find work."

"What about me?" Teddy asked. "What about me and all the stuff we've done this summer? And the summer ain't over yet. So, what about us and Ann?"

"She make her own fate. You make your own fate. I makes Pee Wee's fate."

"Interesting," Lone Wolf said. "I'll make a deal with you Pee Wee—"

"You may call me Hattie, on account of that's my business name."

"Hattie, then." Lone Wolf chuckled. "Go home. If you don't find what you need there, come back when the leaves are starting to turn. You can come back and work here with me. I make this promise to you, and I won't break it. But now, I need for you to go home. For a girl to cry like you did for her pa, I imagine he was a great man. Maybe he didn't want you to live your life in the woods. Maybe he wanted to see you do things in the world."

Pee Wee stared at him. A tear rolled down her cheek. "Pa said that little people do the biggest things. He said I was small, but I sure made up for it in stature. Whatever that means."

"It means you have bigger things to do than talk to an Indian about life." Lone Wolf smiled. "Maybe you should go home and write about your pa. Keep his memories and tell him about any new ones. He is still here, you know."

"How you know? You got the sight too?"

Lone Wolf glanced at Teddy. "I am not like you and Teddy. I don't have magical powers to see things. What I mean is that your pa is around here in spirit. He moves through the trees, he's the wind that hugs you when you run, he's everywhere. He is the love that surrounds you."

"I like you, Mister Wolf."

"Go home, Hattie. Write down all the good things you remember about your pa. Think about my words, and you can always come back if you ever need to talk. I'm real good at listening."

"You done took up a lot of his time," Teddy said, walking over to the doorway. "Let's get you home. Your ma is probably worried sick. If that's okay with you?"

Pee Wee sighed. "Thanks, Mister Wolf. Sorry I took your time up."

"Your ma is probably worried sick 'bout you," Teddy said. "Is that okay? We can go now."

Teddy waved goodbye to Lone Wolf.

She and Pee Wee made their way down the path toward the bridge. By the time they reached the community garden, on their way toward the bridge, the sun was high in the sky, shining down on them and warming their skin.

"He sweet on you." Pee Wee laughed while they strolled.

"Speakin' of sweet…" Teddy pointed ahead at the community garden, where Bump and Ann were harvesting vegetables.

"Bump like Ann. He nasty. Always got snot on his face." Pee Wee stuck her tongue out at them as they passed by.

"Next time, don't come back!" Ann yelled at Pee Wee.

"Yeah, leave all the real ladies for me, Pee Wee!" Bump yelled. "I saw some gators out there, hungry for ya."

Pee Wee waved them off and kept walking. "See, told ya."

"All that can change, but now I need to talk to ya serious." They reached the bridge, where Teddy stopped and sat on a log. "I can't teach you no more rootwork. Your ma wanna leave this place. Ya gotta go with her, Pee Wee. After what I'm doin' tonight…I gotta be real careful. Start movin' around again too."

"Why?"

"You'll see, but white folk don't never forget nothin'. I may go back North." She stared off at the horizon.

"Sound like you don't wanna leave here either."

Teddy glanced at her and smiled. "I don't. But I make my own destiny. Maybe I'll stay. I don't know."

"I thought adults had all the answers," Pee Wee mumbled.

"Did your ma and pa ever tell you 'bout Miss Dot and her daughter, Everly?"

"I don't think they tell me much of nothin.'"

"Well, I'm gonna tell you. Miss Dot was one of the first to live here. She had a daughter… You ever see a porcelain doll?"

"I saw one in a book, I think."

"Everly looked like a porcelain doll—skin was the color of cream and so soft. At least, that's what I hear. She was what they called 'headstrong.' That means she was kinda like you: didn't want nobody plannin' nothin' for her.

"But her ma, Miss Dot, had big dreams for Everly. She put her in a good finishin' school, she taught her all these languages, and she did a lot of stuff because she knew it would be good for Everly. I hear she even told her, 'You gonna be my ticket outta here.'"

"What's that mean?" Pee Wee asked.

"See, Miss Dot had a plan. She was gonna take Everly to this real fancy party in town for girls like her, mixed girls. She was gonna have Everly meet some real fine rich man and take them both away. He would marry Everly, and Miss Dot would go live with them. Only one person didn't know about the plan."

"Everly?"

"Yep, Everly. She had already met someone. He was a Cajun boy. His family would cook for everyone sometimes, because they caught the best rabbits and turtles around. I remember

Pa told me once that they food was so spicy he spent a week wiping his butt with peppermint leaves."

Pee Wee and Teddy laughed. "That sound like my pa."

"That boy's name was Gabriel, I think. So, he was comin' through the village one day and saw Everly. I hear that when they looked at each other, everything was silent. Even the air stopped moving, until he said somethin' like, 'You sure is pretty as a picture' And she smiled back at him. He kept gushing until Miss Dot came out and run him off.

"But he sneaked back that night and asked for her to meet him somewhere. And she did. And they kept meeting in secret until it was almost time for the big ball. Everly let Miss Dot fix her up in a nice dress and everything, but she told her ma that she didn't wanna go, because wouldn't meet nobody that would love her like Gabriel.

"Miss Dot had a fit. She was yellin' and cussin', but she still had to go to town and get some final stuff for her dress. She told Everly that she best change her mind by the time she come back. Everly didn't change her mind. She didn't want to stay here either. She wanted to make her own way with Gabriel, not go to some stupid ball and meet some man that would take her somewhere she don't know. So, while Miss Dot was gone, Everly saw the voodoo lady."

"Oh, her house caught fire. That lady? I think I seen her in the woods before."

Ann and Bump walked up the trail toward the bridge, where Teddy and Pee Wee were sitting. Ann walked over and gave Pee Wee a bunch of strawberries. "By the time you get home, ain't gonna be no more grits. Eat these."

"Ann, I'm sorry 'bout—" Pee Wee started.

"Don't matter. We sisters. We always goin' to be sisters. Don't worry bout nothin'. 'Sides, you was just mad, I'm sure. Right?" Ann's voice pushed Pee Wee into nodding yes.

"I'll tell ma I saw you with Aunt Teddy. Come home when y'all ready." Ann started walking away. Bump lingered and stuck his tongue out at Pee Wee.

"Bump, get on before I start castin'!" Teddy said.

"Strawberries is real sweet." Pee Wee said, with a mouthful. "It's like if God kissed fruit with sunshine."

"So, like I was sayin'," Teddy continued, "Everly went to the voodoo lady and got a sleepin' potion. When her ma came home, Everly made dinner and gave the potion to her. Her ma fell asleep at the table, and Everly and Gabriel moved her to the bed. Then, they left town."

"She seem like she just met him," Pee Wee said.

"Well, true love knows true love. And I'm skippin' a lot because I gotta get you home. But anyway, Everly made her way up North and married Gabriel. She was happier than when she was gonna go to the ball. She came back once and tried to tell her ma, but her ma kept sayin' 'All those years, I gave up everythin' for you to marry a poor boy. This wasn't what you was destined for.'

"And Everly said that she made her own destiny. She was happy with what happened to herself, and besides, she had some real cute babies. She even became a teacher, kinda like her ma, who was a Sunday school teacher, I think. Everly chose what she wanted to do. She made her own destiny.

"Now, I hear about how you been hemmin' and hawin' about this and that. You know, you gonna get a time in your life where you have to choose. You gonna have to make your own destiny. So you can take everything that you gonna learn and leave later—with a head full of knowledge—or you can leave now with a head full of rocks and shovel horse shit all your life. What you wanna do?"

"I wanna live my own way and be happy."

"At ten, do you think you got enough to know how to do that?"

"Well...I..."

Teddy cut her off with a stare. "No. You don't. Look, you not gonna have to do everything everybody want you to do all your life, but you need to let people help get you on the right road. I didn't have anybody to really help me. My brother was gone, my pa was gone, and my ma lost her mind, so she was gone. You got a ma that love you and two sisters that will do anything for you, and you wanna run away and be all grown. Be a ten-year-old for a little longer and just enjoy life. I promise the things you learn will help you be the best Pee Wee you can be. And it'll make your pa real proud."

"I wanna make my own decisions."

"Nobody said you can't. Right now, you need to learn how to make the right decisions before you make all the wrong ones. Understand?"

Pee Wee tossed some leaves from the strawberries over the bridge. "I understand."

"You can't be runnin' off when you don't get whatcha want. My ma woulda tanned my hide if I ran off like you did!" Teddy laughed a bit. "Now I can tell you about how much I love this place. I love all the differences and all the things that are the same. I love steppin' out an catchin' catfish or gettin' beignets from the city on Sundays." Teddy's voice halted. "But we should really get you home."

Pee Wee looked up at her. "I seen how Mister Wolf was lookin' at ya."

"You don't miss a beat, do ya?" Teddy laughed and wiped a few tears from her eyes.

"I's the smartest, that's why I gets the best grades and all the car'mels. I'm gonna try real hard, Teddy. I'm gonna try to learn and listen and stuff, but I really don't wanna leave the parish. If I gotta jump off the wagon and run back here myself."

"Don't put the cart before the horse, Pee Wee." Teddy stood and stretched. "Live day by day, okay. Listen to your ma. Have fun with your sisters. Keep studyin' rootwork and school stuff. When it's time for you to be able to make your own decisions, I know you'll be ready."

"I hears whatcha sayin' and I listen good." Pee Wee got off the log. She stood in front of Teddy. "Like I heard my teacher say, 'I will give it some thought.' Is that okay?"

"Fine by me. Now, let's get you back home."

CEREMONY

Pee Wee, having taken Lone Wolf's advice, sat on her bed, sketching in a book Teddy gave her. Betty and Gene were talking on the front stoop of a neighbor's house, and Ann was outside, folding and putting fresh laundry in a basket from the clothesline, when Ma called to them all.

Pee Wee sighed. "I was really gettin' into this." She tossed the sketch book on her bed and lumbered down the steps. She bumped into Ann, who was bringing the basket of laundry in. Ann set it inside the door.

"Guess we gotta get goin'," she said, tossing the apron she wore on top of the basket. "What was you doin' upstairs?"

"Writin' spells and stuff. I remember some. I'm gonna make my own rootwork book. Teddy ain't the only one that think she smart." Pee Wee said, pulling on her shoes. "She told me I gotta go with ma."

Ann looked down and kicked at an invisible dust ball. "We gotta go, Pee Wee. It's what's right."

"How you know?" Pee Wee snatched the laces on her shoes tight and in anger. "This is all I know. How you know anything?"

"I know Betty asked me to go to school with her…"

Pee Wee made a face at Ann and sighed. "And you say yeah, huh?"

Ann glared at her. "No, I say no."

"Oh." Pee Wee tied the other shoe. "Why? You can stay in the parish that way."

"You know Ma need us since Pa died. She pretend she all right, but she not all right." Ann grabbed a sweater. "Bring you one too. We suppose to be gettin' back way after dark."

"We goin' to see Teddy and do somethin', right?"

"I know about as much." Ann nodded. "Could be fun. Seems like fun stuff happen at night."

"Yeah," Pee Wee moaned. "Like Betty sneakin' off with Gene and gettin' yelled at."

"I heard ya!" Betty ran into the cabin and up the stairs. "Ma say I gotta go tonight. I don't feel like it."

"That's the thing, Betty, you never feel like nothin'. Maybe if it was Gene there…" Ann chided.

"No, that's not it. I just don't like Teddy. She give me a bad feelin', like that idiot that look at you in class all the time but don't say nothin'. Then, you ask if he gotta problem, he laugh or somethin' stupid."

"Sound like Gene." Pee Wee wrapped her arms around herself and pretended to be another person kissing her. Then, she shot a glance at Ann.

"I'm a getcha for that, Pee Wee!" Betty yelled.

"That's why you don't come with us?" Ann asked.

Betty rumbled down the stairs, looked around and lowered her voice. "Y'all ain't mad, are ya? It's just, after Pa died and stuff, I don't even wanna be here. I look round, and all I see is him."

Ann snickered. "Like Pee Wee? Like ghosts?"

"No, idiot! Like Pa waitin' on the porch, or Pa smilin' while he burnin' hoecakes. You know Pa couldn't cook for nothin'." Betty sat on her bed.

"I miss him too, but we can't run away from everything that was Pa. Seem like you wanna forget him. We shouldn't do that. We gotta remember Pa, always." Ann adjusted her dress. "Now come on. Gene comin' with us?"

"Ma said no. He say he'll wait here for us, but I think he gonna sneak and come." Betty beamed. "I do love that boy."

"Lordy." Ann rolled her eyes. "If'n Teddy is part of this, I would tell him to stay back. Never know if she got the third eye or somethin'."

Betty laughed. "Third eye?"

"I don't know. I read 'bout it somewhere. Anyway, tell him to stay here." Ann shuffled down the stairs in front of Betty.

Ma looked up from one of the cabinets, where she had pulled out several lanterns. "We gonna need these to come back. Mister Wolf comin' too."

"The horse Indian?" Pee Wee asked, leaning into the doorway from the porch.

"Yeah, he's just like our direction-man. We ain't goin' to get lost, but Teddy wanna us to be sure to get back."

"What is this? This whole thing is big and secret." Betty grabbed two lamps.

Ma groaned and grabbed some matches. "It's somethin' Teddy think will give us some peace. She say it should help us move on." She stuffed the matches into a huge pocket on the front of her skirt. "But can't nothin' help us move on less that sheriff get his."

They followed Ma out of the house.

Gene sat on the porch in the rocking chair and waved to Betty. "Don't kill nobody, y'all!"

"Skeet comin' to sit with ya," Ma yelled back. "Don't let the place burn down."

"I promise, with all my heart, I will watch it." He grinned, his tanned skin shining in the afterglow of the sun.

"That's what make me nervous," Ma said.

Pee Wee and Ann giggled.

Betty hit them both. "Take these lanterns."

They trudged a ways past the cemetery, and then past Teddy's house, listening to the sounds of sunset get louder the deeper into the forest they went. The bullfrogs called to each other, and things slithered across the muddy path in front of them. Ghosts of runaway slaves led the way to where they were going. The air tasted like nervousness and smelled like cypress trees and Spanish moss.

Ahead were several lamps hidden behind a small town of shacks. Beyond that came the sound of drummers furiously pounding the skins of their dreams, like a beating heart filling the forest with a hollow sound. Ma kept her head raised and walked ahead of the girls. A few people from their village joined them and kept a steady pace behind them.

"I know where we at," Pee Wee said. "We went just past where the…"

Ma shushed her. "We all know where we at. The question is, what is we doin'?"

They made their way to a clearing with torches lit all round. The ground was dry and sparkled brown beneath the flames. People sat in a wide circle on logs, their eyes glowing red with the reflection of fire.

At the front of the gathering were several vertical wooden poles with chains hanging from them. The poles stood over a trough.

"What is—" Betty whispered.

"Thank you for coming," Teddy said, stepping forward from the darkness, sheathed in black, her brown skin glowing like an ember. "I'm surprised to see ya here, Betty. Have a seat right up front."

"Aunt Teddy, what's going on?" Pee Wee asked.

"You'll see. Eat what ya bought, or not. At least drink some water. If'n you need anything, lemme know." Teddy looked up at the sound of horses and a wagon approaching. It was Beaux driving the horses. She turned back to Betty. "Thank you for comin'. You don't know how much this means…to have the sisters…the three of y'all. Thank you so much."

Betty's mouth opened and closed like a fish. No sound escaped her lips while Ma guided her to sit on the log.

"Whatcha think, Pee Wee?" Ann whispered as everyone sat down.

Beaux drove the wagon into the clearing between the spectators and slowed the horses near the poles. Pee Wee saw a figure wriggling around in back of the wagon: very pale and in restraints.

Beaux nodded his head at a few burly men who were standing nearby. They stepped toward the rear of the cart.

The men reached into the wagon and tried to drag out whoever was in there, but the figure fought against them. During the struggle, the crowd got a better look: the figure was white and fought hard. It was naked with black symbols painted all over the body and a hood covering the face. And it had a voice. Everyone leaned forward when the muffled yell rang out. A few people smiled in recognition.

It was the sheriff.

"Oh Lord, what have they done?" Ma whispered. She covered her mouth and looked around, holding her hand to her chest. "Sweet Jesus, what have they done?"

Betty grabbed some water, and Ann munched on a piece of bread.

"All of y'all that's been wronged know who this is," Beaux yelled over the mumbling crowd. "All of y'all know, we gonna get what we deserve. He done killed too many folks I know. Too many people in my life lost lives to this man!"

The crowd watched as someone chained the sheriff to the poles behind him.

A man dressed in black from head to toe stepped forward as a child came to lead the horses and wagon away. "Most of y'all know me, but everybody in town call me Preacher." He held a Bible in the air. "Now, we all know that we was wronged by this man! He think he can take your land, if'n he can't burn ya off it! He scare your chillin' and make babies with ya wife cause he wanna." The man preached like it was the end of time, fire and brimstone seemed to shoot from his mouth as he spoke. His vitriol filled the air and infected some of the people on the logs. "He think he can take everything from all of us that ain't got nothin'. We gonna show him...we gonna show the whole damned town that we tired of all this! We tired of them botherin' us!"

"Preach! Preach!" someone yelled.

The girls glanced at Ma, who still held her hand over her heart, breathing heavily but listening attentively.

"We goin' to let them know, not tonight!" the preacher yelled. "No more! None of this! And ya know what? We goin' to get us a black sheriff to take his place! A black one, dark as night and smart as anything!" Preacher waved his Bible in the air. "It says here, in the good book, 'Eye for an eye, tooth for tooth, hand for hand, foot for foot, burn for burn, wound for wound, stripe for stripe!' Does it not say that in Exodus?"

Ma went from gasping and covering her mouth to raising her hand and waving it. She yelled, "Yes! Yes, Lord!"

"And does it not say that after Peter asked Jesus, 'Lord, how many times shall I forgive my brother or sister who sins against me? Up to seven times?' And what does Jesus say? 'Seventy-seven times.' Now, I look around at all these people, and I see more than seventy-seven times of forgiveness! I see more than one hundred times of forgiveness, and I see that we shall take vengeance in our hands to keep these white people from comin' in here and stealin' from us! From beatin' us in the town! From callin' out our names! From feelin' safe around this man that lets them do all the things they do!"

"Cut the head off the snake!" someone yelled. "Cut it off! Burn the neck, and no snake should take its place!"

Teddy walked up close to the preacher and put her hand on his shoulder. "Preacher, I think you got the message across. Now, let's get to doin' what we come to do."

"Sister!" He raised his Bible in the air. "Sister! Thank you for lettin' me speak. Let's get on with it!"

"Some of y'all know who this is, but for those who don't..." Teddy turned and pulled the hood off the man's head. "Let's welcome the sheriff to our little gatherin'!"

The sheriff's eyes widened. His mouth had a gag in it, tied around his head. All he could do was make a muffled sound and try to move his body. His manhood was covered with a piece of cloth, but his skin was painted whiter than white, with dark drawings on it.

Beaux walked over to Betty, Ann, and Pee Wee. "While we get him ready, we ask that y'all lay hands on this knife and pray with me."

"No!" Betty jumped up. "Y'all gonna kill this man?"

Pee Wee snatched the knife. "Do I get to cut him first? He killed my pa."

Ann looked at Pee Wee. "You don't understand what you sayin'."

"I'm not touching nothin'!" Betty sat back on the log and crossed her arms. "Why y'all doin' this?"

Ma leaned forward. "Didn't ya hear, Preacher? This here is the only time you can get your revenge on a bad man. A very bad man. I'm not sayin' it's good or bad. But will it make ya feel better? Maybe next time you look round town and see how many of them kids got black mamas and papas and white skin, maybe that'll change your mind. This man done bad things, I tell ya! He didn't get me no justice for my husband, who was a good man! Helped most of y'all when ya needed somethin', if'n he was around. I deserve justice for my girls! The little dead babies deserve justice! If'n you don't do nothin', what you want if'n his folk come for you? Turn around, and I won't be there!"

"Maybe you should look in a mirror," Ann said to Betty.

"What's that supposed to mean?" Betty asked.

Ann shrugged and glanced at Ma before she put her hands on the blade, and Pee Wee gripped the handle, but Betty refused to touch it.

She started to stand again, but Ma put one hand on her, sitting her down, and the other on the knife. "Can you use my hand?"

"We need the girls," Beaux said. "We really need all the girls. More powerful."

Ma wrapped an arm around Betty and held her. "You gonna do this for me. You owe it to your pa. Do it for him, too. This man is a bad man." She reached behind Betty and tried to force her hand forward. Betty pulled her hands in tight and tried to wrap them around herself until Ann reached over and grabbed Betty's hand.

"Can we do it this way?" Ann asked.

Pee Wee turned the knife toward Betty. "All my life I ain't never asked you for nothin'. Do this, and you'll never have to ask me nothin' again."

A lightning bolt crackled in the sky and punctuated the ground near Pee Wee. She stumbled backwards and fell to the ground. A small circle of sparks appeared around them on the ground and changed to low flames.

Betty jumped in fright and moved away from Pee Wee and the others. "Pee Wee, you just mad."

Pee Wee's eyes shone like coals with small red flames dancing in them. "I'm mad, but this man killed my pa, and I want this done, whatever it is."

A mist slowly rolled in and surrounded the girls—Betty, Ann, and Pee Wee.

Pee Wee spread her arms and welcomed the white fog surrounding them. She chanted, "Come...come...come..."

Betty bit her tongue.

Pee Wee glanced at Ann, whose eyes were wide with a combination of fear and awe. She watched Ann whisper for Betty to pay attention.

Betty fought harder until she saw the look on Pee Wee's face. Then she calmed herself. She didn't fight as hard as she had been, but she remained rigid and stood her ground.

The flames around them shot higher and burned brighter. The crowd of people silenced.

"Do it!" Pee Wee yelled in a voice that was not her own.

Ann jumped and glanced at Pee Wee. "You okay?"

Pee Wee stretched her arms above her head. A bolt of lightning seemed to fly from her hands and into the trees. The people around Pee Wee cheered, and some women raised their hands and shouted words of praise.

Ann fell back and grabbed Teddy. "Do somethin'! How she doin' that? Where that lightning come from! Teddy, do somethin'!" Ann whispered. "Make her stop! She done lost her mind!"

Teddy grinned. "She got the spirits in her. She fine."

Ma raised her hands and yelled thanks to the sky. Some women around them broke out into cries of "amen" and "Thank you, Jesus."

Pee Wee pointed a finger at the knife. "Put the hand on the knife, child," Pee Wee said to Betty, but not in Pee Wee's voice.

Teddy nodded her head and laughed—high and shrill. "Now, she sound like her pa. Put your hand on the knife, girl."

"Why?" Betty cried.

"Because it's more powerful. 'Sides, we not gonna kill him," Teddy reassured her.

"We not?" Betty asked. "What is we gonna do?"

"We gonna take his skin." Teddy hummed a hymn as she grinned and pulled Betty's hand toward the knife.

When Betty placed her hand on the knife, Ann did too.

Teddy stepped forward and wrapped black ribbons around the girls' wrists. They held the knife, and a strong wind rose, and lifted all three up off the ground.

"It's your ancestors thankin' ya." Teddy glanced at each of them as new-found energy filled her, and her hands moved like spiders with the ribbon.

Ma gasped. "I can smell your pa. He sittin' right here, next to me!"

Up in the air, Pee Wee's body seized, her eyes rolling back in her head. Betty inhaled sharply, blindly reaching for Ann, who placed her free hand on Betty's arm.

Everyone watched as the three girls floated higher into the air. A presence seemed to hold them up, but the crowd beneath them swooned in rapturous glory and continued singing and shouting "amen."

Pee Wee let out a loud scream as her body arched backwards so much that her head seemed to touch her feet. Betty and Ann gripped each of her arms, screaming along with her. Although Pee Wee seemed in rapture, Betty and Ann were in full fear.

"What is happening to her?" Betty shrieked, but Ann only gave her a look of terrified confusion.

Pee Wee straightened up and looked at them both.

"What?" she asked, in her own voice.

Their bodies all crashed to the ground and collapsed into a pile.

Teddy took the ribbon and the knife from the girls. The crowd of people glanced around while the mist curled back into the trees.

Ma sat on the log, rocking back and forth, hugging herself. "Thank you."

Teddy grinned. "Thank *you.*"

When Teddy, carrying the knife, walked over to where the sheriff was chained to the poles, the woman washing his back with warm water stepped away. Teddy picked up a piece of charcoal and redrew the lines on his body. Then she stabbed one of them and gently slid the blade beneath his skin.

Blood poured from the cut, and the sheriff hollered into the gag. His body tensed as Teddy maneuvered the knife around, until she had cut off a huge piece of skin from his back.

The sheriff's head fell forward, his body limp. Someone swiped something under his nose and revived him.

Beaux took the flap of skin from her and placed it on some paper. "You gonna need more," he said. "Try taking it from the thigh this time, chéri." He placed a bucket next to her.

They all stared as Teddy set to work, cutting pieces of skin off the man and dropping them into the bucket. Beaux stroked the first piece of skin and devilishly glanced at Teddy.

"The first always the best, chéri.," he crooned.

"That's why I been practicin' since the last time." Teddy said as she slipped the knife beneath the sheriff's skin.

Betty leaned forward and threw up all the water she'd been drinking.

Pee Wee laughed and spoke in a voice that was not hers. Ann kept a heavy grip on Pee Wee's shoulder.

Betty dropped to her knees, wiping her mouth with the back of her hand.

Lone Wolf appeared out of the darkness and walked over and helped her to her feet. "Chew this," he whispered, and gave her a handful of leaves and part of a white root of ginger. "This will help you."

"Thanks," she mumbled and took the ginger root. She sucked on it as he led her away from the scene. "Where you been at?"

"I am always around. You may not see me, but I'm always there." He placed a comforting arm around her shoulders.

"Well, on account a what's happenin', seems 'bout right."

Lone Wolf looked back and nodded his head. "This can be a bit much."

"You seen anything like this before?"

Lone Wolf glanced back once more but didn't answer her question., "Are you ready to head home?" His voice was soft over the drumming and the chanting and the screaming of the sheriff. "I can take you there now."

"Please. I can't…I can't…" Her voice shook as she leaned on him.

Mister Wolf chuckled. "They can never handle the first one. After a few of these, you will be fine."

Betty gaped at him.

He smiled. "I thought that would make you laugh a bit."

"I just watched a man get peeled. His skin was peeled from his body, and you say that 'after the first one'…? I can't get outta here fast enough."

Teddy finished, dropping the last hunk of skin from the sheriff's thigh into the bucket with the other pieces. She rinsed her hands off and gave the knife to Beaux.

He nodded, grabbed the bucket, and walked over to Ma, Pee Wee, and Ann.

"Y'all can go on home. You don't need to see this part," Teddy said.

"But we done seen everything else! I wanna stay!" Pee Wee crossed her arms on her chest. "Ma, you can go."

"I don't think you need to see what's happenin' next, chéri." Beaux held his hand out to help her to stand.

Pee Wee looked around. "I don't feel so good."

"What happened to her?" Ann asked. "Why she sound like a million people livin' inside of her?"

"Some of us can get taken over by other spirits pretty easy," Teddy said. "Since she can see 'em, maybe they can get inside her easier."

Pee Wee stumbled a bit before she fell. Beaux caught her with one arm as he passed the bucket of bloody skin to Teddy with his other. "C'mon now, let's get ya home."

"How long before it's ready?" Teddy asked Beaux.

"Two, maybe three, days. I got it all set up and can start tomorrow."

Ma and Ann followed Beaux and Teddy, but then Ma stopped walking. "I'll stay behind. I'll be fine."

Ann stopped. "Are you sure?"

"You don't know what this man done. This sheriff." Ma spat.

"No, I don't know, on account of nobody tellin' me nothin'." Ann crossed her arms.

"You listen to me." Ma moved close enough that Ann felt her rage burning off her body. Ma lowered her voice to a whisper. "You know Skeet had a sister? You know he would come and sneak her outta school and do things to her. Bad things, 'til she jumped into the river. She was maybe fourteen.

"Now, if ya think about how many times he done this same thing. And even how many times he let his boys do the same thing and watch, you understand why I wanna stay here. This bigger than him lettin' your pa die. It's much bigger." Ma stepped back. She groaned as she sat back on the log. "Leave the wagon. I'll pull it back."

"Oh," Ann whispered. "Okay."

Teddy turned and walked toward the crowd of people. She raised her bloody hands into a V for victory, a triumphant night. The blood of the sheriff rolled from her fingertips down to beneath her arms. Teddy swiped the air with the knife, and the crowd hungrily cheered.

"Y'all want more?" Teddy shouted before passing the knife to the woman who drew on the sheriff. "More?"

The woman loosened the gag and forced his mouth open. She chanted something rhythmic while the drums pounded in time with the crowd's yells for *more*. She reached in and cut his tongue out of his mouth.

"We take this tongue and offer it up..." she shouted.

"We offer it up to you, Father God!" Preacher snatched the tongue and threw it into the fire. "We offer the burnt tongue of this sinner up to you!"

The crowd roared with approval. The sound of a whip cracked in the air.

Preacher raised his Bible. "Fun times 'bout to start folks! Ya see...the Lord says..."

His voice drifted further from Ann and Pee Wee as they headed home.

BETTY

When we got home, I see Gene sittin' on the porch with Skeet. Lone Wolf gestured for me to go on ahead and began walkin' back the way we came.

"Thanks, Lone Wolf, sir!" I yelled, watchin' him walk away.

They got lanterns lit all over and it looks kinda like the inside of a pumpkin or somethin'. All orange and glowy lookin', with the moon shinin' down, and when I step up onto the porch, Gene say I look like I done seen a ghost. He holds a lantern up to my face and wipes the tears off my cheek with his other hand.

"I seen things that I don't wanna see no more." I ignored Skeet askin' a question or somethin' and grabbed Gene's wrist. "Come on upstairs and help me get packed."

Upstairs, out of breath, I lay on my bed for a few minutes. Then I told Gene what we did—what I saw—and how everybody was okay with skinnin' a white man while he was alive.

"You want me to light another lantern?" He sat on the floor next to my bed.

"Sure, and then I want you to yell out the window that I'm here!" I snapped. "Don't light no light. We can see fine. Moon's bright enough over here."

He shifted his weight and crossed his legs.

I crossed my arms on my chest and looked up at the ceiling. I could see Pa in the woodwork. I could hear him poundin' nails and tellin' us how big this room goin' to be. All I see is him everywhere I look.

"Sheriff is a bad man." Gene looked down. "I mean, my ma say that you reap what you sow."

I looked at him and felt like my face was on fire. "Who are we to do this? That man ain't never done me no harm. Yeah, he ain't do nothin' 'bout killin' my pa. And when he stopped us in the city, I thought he was jokin', but really, he ain't do much of nothin'. Then, Ann gonna say—"

"What she say?" Gene sat next to me and grabbed my hand. "What she say? She agree with you?"

"She say that maybe I should look into a mirror." Even when I said it out loud, I heard the sound of my heart breakin'. Like nobody thought none of this was strange, but then for her to say that I could be the sheriff's...

"You are kinda light-bright. Not red-bone, but you really could pass easier than your sisters." Gene's voice low, like a whisper. I could hardly hear him. "You mean, you never thought about it?"

I opened my mouth to say somethin', but all I could do was hiccup. Then I did it again. My face felt hot. I looked around the room at Pee Wee's bed and then at Ann's. I heard them jumping back and forth from each other's beds when we was little. How Ann made fun of my mosquito net but used it all the time.

My good boots for ridin' was in the corner. Thinkin' about how I lost my horse when Ma caught me smokin'. I went and picked them up. I grabbed two suitcases from behind the dresser, next to the boots.

Lone Wolf was right. Pa is all around us. He's in this house, every part of it. He's in this dresser. He's in this floor, and I feel him inside me, in my heart.

And he tellin' me that I gotta go.

Gene kept talkin', but I started grabbing stuff and packin'. I only took what was mine. My pants and skirts, stupid drawings of stuff Pee Wee made and gave to me. On the dresser was one picture. It was the only picture we had of all three of us. I wanted to take it. I picked it up and the frame felt so heavy.

We was young, didn't know much of nothin' in this picture. Pee Wee laughin', Ann tryin' not to smile, and me laughin' with Pee Wee. Ma was real mad cuz she paid good money for that man to take the picture. He give it to us for free cuz he said he couldn't do nothin' with it no way.

"You gonna take it?" Gene walked up behind me and put his hand on the frame. "Or you gonna leave it?"

"I—I don't know." I felt shaky and hot, but I wanted to get out of there so bad.

"Then put it down and let's go." Gene's voice sounded real nice in my ear. "I been thinkin' that you can stay with me and Ma, or at the store. Don't matter, I just want ya to be happy. You ain't been happy all summer."

"I just been thinkin' that I'm ready to go. Ma done paid the school and—"

"And maybe the school can take you early. Not like they don't have space. I mean, you s'pose to start in a month…"

Gene kept talkin'. Seem like everythin' he sayin' is what was in my head already. I set the picture down and finished packin' by moonlight. I knew where all my stuff was anyway. Not like I been here but to sleep the last few days.

He ran over and looked out a window. "I'm seein' torches. They all probably comin' home. You ready to go? Whatcha gonna do?"

For a minute, I didn't know what to do. I was mad, and I felt like nobody understood what I was tryin' to say. If I left, I would lose half my soul—my sisters. If I go, I ain't comin' back.

But they skinned that man. They took his skin like nothin' and God knows what else. All this ain't start 'til Teddy come round.

I dropped the last of my stuff in the suitcase. "Let's go. I ain't never comin' back."

Gene grabbed the suitcases and we ran down the stairs. Skeet was on the porch, talkin' to someone, but I didn't care. This was gonna be a new life. Maybe I can get in the finishin' school and figure out how to make money so I can stay there.

All's I know is that once I jump across this threshold, my life will change.

Gene looked up at me from the bottom of the steps. "If you comin', let's go!"

I rested my hand on the doorway and looked back one last time. All my times here wasn't all that bad. Always seem bad when you wanna make it look bad. I saw Pa sittin' on the edge of his bed, gettin' ready to go find work. Ma by the door in her work clothes. Pee Wee and Ann playin' around the table, washin' dishes and stuff. It wasn't all bad.

"Let's go." I reached for Gene's hand and jumped off the steps.

🍂 PEE WEE

Yesterday, when we got home, Betty was gone. Ma wasn't surprised. Ma said that she was goin' to town to look for her. She even went to that finishin' school, and they said she wasn't there. But Ma said she left the money she paid, so Betty could go if she wanted.

I stared out the window at the sun comin' up. Birds sure sound happy when you is sad. Why can't everything be sad because I'm sad?

I heard Ann movin' around in her bed and woke her up.

"So, she gone," I said to Ann.

Ann was half sleep and sat up. "She gone."

"Was it me?"

"Whatcha mean?"

"Well, when we went to the thing with Teddy, I felt strange. Like I was outta my body, lookin' at my body, but somebody else was in my body."

"Nuh-uh." The scarf she slept in had come off last night, and she look like a scarecrow or somethin'. She tried to fix her hair. "I figure somethin' happened. You ain't sound like you."

"Whatchu mean? I ain't sound like me? I can't remember everything but some stuff I know happened." I said.

"Like what?" Ann asked.

"Like fallin' down," I said. "I saw Lone Wolf and he was far away. Felt like I was flyin', but had to be a dream. I know they cut that man up. Got no problem with that, after what he done to our pa."

"Was you scared?"

"Scared of what? Felt like a dream. I don't know much of what happened. Like I said!" What is she talkin' 'bout? She makin' me kinda mad.

Ann looked at me. "Was you? I know you, Pee Wee. You always gonna be Pee Wee. You could be...I dunno...that Queen of France, and when I see you, you just Pee Wee."

"I saw myself cuttin' that white man and him screamin'. I even heard his voice in my head askin' why they doin' this to him."

"For real? That's somethin'." Ann stood up and fixed her nightgown. "Well, I would love to keep talkin', but nature calls. Whatcha doin' today?"

"I dunno. Maybe stay here. Help with the chores. Ma seem like somethin' kinda off." I felt a lil sad for Ma. She looked everywhere for Betty. Skeet been askin' round but ain't seen nothin'.

I hear the door downstairs open and close. Ma callin' up to see if we up. She sound real tired. Ann done ran down to go to the bathroom, and I run down and look at Ma.

"Betty's probably in town. I hope she at least go to that school." Ma flopped down in a chair, "Hattie, help me take off my shoes. Patricia Ann, can you put some water on for tea?"

"Why you callin' her by her whole name?" I asked. "'Sides, she went outside to go pee."

Ma's feet was real hot in them shoes. She went lookin' in her work shoes cuz they the best kind for walkin'.

"Huh?" Ma looked at me. She looked like she was asleep. "Oh, I don't know. Sometimes, I see you as my Hattie..."

"Ma...Pee Wee. Y'all know I like it cuz it's what Pa called me."

Ma smiled, real warm, and closed her eyes. "We gotta get packin' in the next week or so. I hear a storm's comin'. And I just really wanna get as far away from here as possible."

"What about Teddy?"

But Ma didn't say nothing, cuz she was already asleep.

The rest of the day, I didn't do much of nothin'. Bump came over and we talked on the porch. He'd heard that Betty left, but didn't know where she'd gone. He said Gene and his horses was gone too.

"Well, Bump, she ain't like Teddy much," I said, puttin' my bare foot on the porch rail. "And after that other stuff, I'm not surprised. Like she wanted a reason to go."

Summer felt so lazy that afternoon that even the wind had a hard time blowin'. But, we just sat there like old folks do, and did nothin'. Ann was doin' somethin' all day. Maybe laundry, I don't know. I just wanted to sit out there and think about nothin'. Even when Ma got up to make dinner, me and Bump just sat out on that porch. She gave us permission to eat out there, and we did.

Then I saw Teddy strollin' down the path.

"Teddy!"

"Pee Wee! Think you and Ann can come by day after next? I got somethin' for ya." She walked up to the porch, just like the day, long and lazy.

"Sure. Why not?" I said.

Teddy sat on the step. Bump stood to leave, but Teddy motioned for him to sit down.

"I heard 'bout Betty," Teddy said. She pulled out a pipe and packed it full of somethin' that smelled sweet.

"Yeah. I think she just was lookin' for a reason to go," I said before I knew I said it.

"That's rather grown of you," Teddy said.

Ma opened the door and stuck her head out. "Teddy, you comin' inside?"

Teddy smiled a bit. "You forgot to call me 'swamp rat.'"

"Nah, I called you a swamp rat in my head. I'm just puttin' on airs for the kids." Ma held the door open. "You want me to fix you a plate?"

Ma's bein' real nice to Teddy. Betty done left. I have a feelin' the world's 'bout to end or somethin'.

 ANN

I can't believe I's scared of my own sister. Not Betty, but Pee Wee. She actin' like she don't remember nothin' that happened days ago. I see everythin' in my head, playin' over and over until I start havin' dreams about it. Then, when I wake up, everythin' remind me of that night. Look like blood in the water I'm washin' dishes in. Or the insides of the chickens I'm cuttin' look like that man.

I couldn't help no one get the hogs ready for slaughter because I kept bein' sick everywhere, seein' that white man screaming like he was dying.

Pee Wee walk around like not much happened. She say she don't remember, but I know she do. She have to. I don't care, but she have to.

I started sleepin' on the couch, and a few days after that she asked me, "Why don't you sleep upstairs no more?"

"I—I just can't look at Betty's empty bed," I lied.

"Oh." Pee Wee knew the real reason why, but she didn't want to say it… "You scared of me."

"No—no, not scared. I guess it's time for me to leave this place. I feel like it just sucked everythin' outta me. All I got, I done gave, and I got nothin' else." I looked at her and somethin' inside me felt broke.

She started to say somethin' but I just said, "I'll be back."

I walked outside and walked around the village. Now that we been back a few days, everythin' look different. It all feel different too. Like heavier or more lonely. I don't know what it is, but I feel like I gotta leave this place.

I saw so many kids playin' and hollerin'. Half of 'em looked mixed with some white. I's filled with sadness and regret. I shoulda never have told Betty to look at herself. My stomach filled with a feelin' so sad that it pulled me down in the dirt.

"Why you look like that?" Bump stopped from runnin' somewhere and ran up to me. "Somebody steal your toys or somethin'?"

"I ain't got no toys, Bump," I said, walkin' toward the bridge to the community garden. "I's just a bit sad. I miss my sister."

Bump bounced alongside me. "Smells strange round here."

I lifted up and smelled the air. "Smells like rain. That's what we need here. A good rain to cleanse this whole place. To wash away all the sin and all the bad feelings—what adults call 'guilt.'"

"Did ya do somethin' bad, Ann?"

"I don't think I did." I know I can't tell Bump nothin' bout the ceremony we had cuz he's little and I don't wanna scare him. I shrug and sigh. "I guess it's been a bad summer, and I'm kinda the one that made it that way. Shouldn't have said my sisters could go see Teddy. Then Pa died, and that business with the sheriff…"

I sat on a hay bale by the edge of the bridge, dropped my face into my hands, and cried like a lost babe.

Bump stood in front of me. "Aw, Ann, it's gonna be fine. I'm a find Betty and get her back here and make you happy again."

Lookin' at him, I realized he was dead serious.

"Bump, let it be. Let sleepin' dogs lie." I motioned him away with my hand. "'Sides, none of us wanna be here. Ma say we leavin' soon. I guess I gotta get back to pack my stuff."

He sat next to me. "So, you goin'?"

I nodded.

"That makes me sad." He looked at his hands. "Maybe I can come with you."

"Bump, I don't think so."

"Ain't nothin' here for me. Don't know my ma or my pa. All I know is Skeet and y'all and some other kids. I likes to talk to the Indian."

I listened to Bump's voice trail off. He's talking about a lot of things. Things I don't wanna know. A raindrop hit me on the head. Then another and another.

I jumped up and smiled. "Bump! I was gonna run over to the garden. You wanna come?"

He stopped talkin' and looked at me. "Yeah, Ann."

I grabbed my skirt and pulled it up over my knees. "Race ya!"

GOODBYE

"**W**hy don't y'all go say your farewells to your Aunt Teddy tomorrow," Ma said over dinner of crawfish and potatoes.

Pee Wee pushed boiled potatoes around on her plate.

Ann glanced at Pee Wee before she finished off a few crawfish. "Real good tonight, Ma."

"Thanks, baby." Ma grabbed a piece of bread and ran it around her plate, sopping up the juice from the crawfish. "Not as spicy as they normally make it."

"Oh, you got this from the…uh…." Pee Wee started.

"They brought it over and told me they ain't seen your sister. I think they lyin', but can't do much a nothin'." Ma wiped her fingers on a wet napkin.

"Is that good?" Ann asked.

"Dunno," Ma responded.

"I just thought of somethin'!" Pee Wee blurted. "You called her Aunt Teddy! Not swamp rat! This mean you like her now?"

"I guess I did." Ma chuckled. "Don't mean nothin' much, Pee Wee."

"Could be. Could be that…I dunno…maybe we can stay with her," Pee Wee added, hoping Ma would agree. "We don't have to leave the parish."

Ma pressed her hands on the table and groaned as she stood. "Ah, Pee Wee. We gotta go, baby. I mean, look out there. It's been rainin' for a few days. I done used some of that funeral money to hire us a person to come get us and take us. He goin' to be here tomorrow."

"Oh." Pee Wee looked down at her food. "I'm not real hungry."

"I know you wanna stay, but we gotta do this. It's gonna be good for us all, I promise." She walked over and hugged Pee Wee. "You gonna have new friends, and we gonna have us a bigger house where we got our own garden and space for chickens. You could even get a dog or somethin'."

"A dog," Pee Wee said.

"A dog!" Ann yelped. "That would be great!"

"A dog." Pee Wee pushed back from the table. "Excuse me, ma'am, I'm going to bed without the rest of my dinner."

"If that's what you want to do." Ma reached down and picked up Pee Wee's plate. "You sure you don't want the rest of the potatoes or anythin'? I'll make a lil stew and have Ann bring you up a bowl later. We gotta eat the last of all this. Not tryin' to take much food with us."

"Um, I'll take the stew, please." Pee Wee said. "It's not like I can go anywhere cuz of that rain. It ain't never stoppin'. Kinda like God is cryin' with me."

Ann jumped up. "God ain't—"

Ma raised a hand. "It's okay, Ann. It has been rainin' pretty bad. I hope y'all can get over there and back. We gonna leave, maybe early afternoon. Dependin' on the rain."

"We just about finished," Ann said. "Nothin' upstairs but mattresses. Everythin' we takin' is down here. Just one more night upstairs."

While Ann cleared the table of the few plates, Ma took the remaining food and dumped it in a pot on the stove. "Always taste better the second day."

A knock at the door made them pause. "Who is it?" Ma asked.

"It's Skeet, dammit! And my arthritis is killin' me!"

Ann rushed and opened the door, revealing Skeet and Bump. Pee Wee sat on the steps and stared.

Skeet passed her umbrella to Bump, who shook it out and stepped inside. They both took off their rain boots.

Skeet handed a bag to Ann. "My goin' away gift."

"Oh! Is it..." Ann pulled out a jar with cloudy white liquid inside. "What's this?"

"Moonshine." Bump shook the remaining water off him. "Skeet wanna have one more drank with y'all."

Ann passed the bottle to Ma. She took Skeet and Bump's rain jackets and shook them out.

"Why you over here?" Bump sat next to Pee Wee on the step.

"We leavin' tomorrow. How is I s'pose to be?"

"I'll miss ya," he whispered.

"I'm not goin' nowhere," Pee Wee mumbled.

"Are you sure? I mean, I thought you was leavin'."

Pee Wee glared at him. He shrugged his shoulders.

Bump jumped off the step and ran over to Ann. "You need help? Since y'all leavin', I gotta get all my time in with ya. This way, when you come back lookin' for me and I'm all man, you gonna fall in love with me."

Ann snorted. "Serious?"

Bump put his hands on his hips and nodded.

"Child, hush!" Ma passed a small jar with some of the moonshine in it to Skeet. "Ann, you want some? I mean, it's a toast..."

"A toast to new adventures!" Skeet laughed. "You can write to ol' Skeet 'bout it, and I'll make Bump read them letters to me."

"Oh, I can read real good!" Bump puffed his chest.

Pee Wee slid up the stairs. She sat on the mattress on the floor before spying her hand-drawn rainbows in the corner from a long time ago. Somethin' she did with Betty and Ann. She looked out the window at the rain pouring down, drenching the land around them. She eyed a path through the trees.

"I'm on my way, Teddy." Pee Wee whispered. "I just gotta wait for them to get to drinkin'."

Pee Wee watched Ma and Skeet snoring on the mattresses on the floor, passed out after drinking the moonshine. Bump lay on the extra mattress, half-asleep, watching Ann sleeping.

Pee Wee maneuvered between them all, grabbed her boots and a plastic bag before she slid outside onto the porch. She pulled on her boots, her knobby knees exposed beneath a pair of shorts and a plastic bag she fashioned into a rain jacket.

Bump sat up and looked at her. He opened his mouth to speak, but she cut him off: "I'm goin' to the bridge by the crops," she whispered. "Tryin' to get one last look before I go."

Pee Wee stepped off the porch. The water had made the land squishy, and mud rose to the top of her rain boots.

It was the sound of the rain that made everything seem peaceful, despite the turmoil she felt brewing inside her. School felt like it had just ended, and with Pa dead and Betty gone, nothing felt right.

"I don't know if we runnin' from problems into more problems or what!" Pee Wee mumbled. Her wet hair had blocked her eyes, and she reached blindly for a tree. She wiped her hair from her eyes. "If'n I had my way, I'd stay here by myself."

When she reached Teddy's place, she saw lights on and heard music playing. People were howling and yelling with laughter. She wasn't sure what was happening, but she needed to get up there.

She struggled to pull her boots from the thick mud as she walked. She cursed under her breath every gooshy step of the way.

"Surprised to see you out here in the rain," a voice to her right said, and Lone Wolf stepped forward from beneath a tree near Teddy's porch and lit a pipe of tobacco. He was dressed in a white T-shirt and a pair of dark slacks.

"I came to say goodbye. We's leavin' tomorrow."

"I know." He puffed a few times then blew a cloud of smoke out.

"Why you here? I mean, downstairs?" Pee Wee shook the rain off and huddled next to him beneath the eaves of the house.

"Sometimes I don't like being around a lot of people. Your aunt has some pretty wild get-togethers, if that's what you want to call them."

"You sure sweet on her, ain't ya?"

Lone Wolf puffed on the pipe and looked off in the distance. He half-smiled. "I suppose you could say I am."

"That's what I thought." Pee Wee crossed her arms. "How much longer you think this rain gonna be?"

"Well, could go all night. Could end any minute. I just like to keep an eye on it. Never know when the levee could break or a flood or somethin'. I mean, Teddy is real close to the water."

"Sounds like a Indian. My pa say—*said*—talkin' to Indians is like talkin' in circles. They go round and round."

Lone Wolf chuckled. "Well, how would your pa know?"

"He works—*worked*—the railroad with Indians. Said he met a Chinese man a couple times, and he met a Jewish man, and a black man that was educated. He go to where the work is." Pee Wee paused. "He *went* to where the work is, I mean."

Lone Wolf smiled and placed his hand on her shoulder. "Well, you can't stay down here all night, little lady. Let's get you upstairs. I'm sure Teddy has something for you to see."

Something swelled inside Pee Wee. All this talking about her pa made her realize that she really and truly missed him with all her heart and soul. "Teddy all I got left of my pa, you know."

"It's hard being the last person standing." Lone Wolf motioned for her to take the ladder upstairs to Teddy's.

Pee Wee stood next to the ladder and looked up at him. "I bet you know what that's like, huh? You's the only one round here. You miss your folks?"

Lone Wolf's bronze skin had a warmth to it as he lit his pipe again. "Let's save that for another day. You should get home soon. I think the levee may flood. Nobody's safe much."

Pee Wee climbed the ladder and sat on the couch while Lone Wolf went inside to speak to Teddy.

A few moments later, Teddy rushed between the party-goers and towards Pee Wee with a box. "I was worried I wasn't gonna see ya! It's ready. I want you to open it and look inside." She set the box on Pee Wee's lap.

Pee Wee grinned. "What is it? Is it for me?"

Teddy raised a finger and told Pee Wee to wait for a sec.

"Goodnight, all!" Teddy waved as the people started to leave out the back of the house. "See y'all next time. Don't forget to leave somethin' for the hostess!"

Lone Wolf picked up a jar of money and walked toward the back of the house. "You heard the lady. She's gotta make a living too."

Pee Wee glanced through the window on the porch and into the house at the people laughing and putting money in the jar Lone Wolf held. She saw white people and black people, maybe even some mixed-race people in there. She listened to people complaining about the rain and the levee. She didn't know much about the levee, nor where it was, but from the way people were talking, it had to be nearby.

But everybody leaving was laughing and having fun, so she didn't worry. She just wanted to be a part of that fun. "This must be like what it is to be an adult." Pee Wee whispered under her breath.

Teddy grabbed a lantern from inside the house and held it near Pee Wee. "The box, open it."

Pee Wee opened the box. Inside was something that smelled like chemicals and varnish. The smell reminded her of when Pa shined his shoes for church, but the thing inside the box was a book, not a shoe. "What's this?" She thumbed through the pages, remembering things she'd seen before. She read spells she knew.

"It's all the rootwork I know. All the stuff y'all did for the summer. It's my going-away gift to you and your sisters. Now you have a piece of Teddy with you when you go."

"But, on the front...what's this? It smell funny." Pee Wee scrunched her nose.

"That is human skin, my dear."

"Human skin?" She snatched her hands back, dropping the book. Her stomach lurched. "Oh man, I don't feel real good, Teddy." She jumped up, ran to one of the screens, and pushed it open. She dry-heaved over the side. "This...this ain't right."

"It's right. I made it right. Now you own something that nobody can take away from you. Ain't no amount of rootwork goin' to fix the spell I put on the sheriff and his whole damn family. He killed your pa. This is what's owed to you. It's what's owed!"

Maybe Betty was right. Maybe this is all wrong, Pee Wee thought as she eased herself back over to the sofa. "Are you sure?"

Teddy nodded. "He killed my brother. You ain't think I'm just gonna let a man like that get away with somethin' stupid? He was my only brother, your only pa..."

"But we got you, Teddy!" Pee Wee yelped.

"And who I got? Huh? Nobody! Your ma gonna take you far away, and I'm gonna be here alone again. I gotcha for a few months outta your life." Teddy kneeled in front of Pee Wee, pushing the box toward her. "Now this...this here is somethin' you can pass down from sister to sister...you can pass it to your children, and they pass it on. You understand? As long as this book is movin' in the family, my name will stay alive... Pa will stay alive. When people stop remembering you, you nothin'. Not even dirt. But long as you got this book, we all can be legendary."

"Legendary?"

"Like a story that's told over and over. You gonna take good care of this and pass it to your sisters. Share the book. That's all my knowledge in there. And you write about the summer on the last pages. I left blank pages in there for all of you."

"Teddy, I don't…" Pee Wee began.

"Help me clean up a bit. This party went on longer than I wanted." Teddy scurried around picking up plates and glasses. She moved a few lanterns around while Pee Wee helped, after she set the package on the couch.

They both stopped when they heard the whinny of a horse and the sound of urgent voices downstairs. It was Lone Wolf, talking to someone in the front of the house.

Moments later, he rushed up the ladder, picked up a pair of binoculars, and stared out the front window, moving them from left to right.

"Just talked to a friend, and he said the levee looks like it's flooding," he said, still looking through the binoculars. "It may not hold."

"That levee been holdin' the waters back forever." Teddy kept cleaning, but Pee Wee kept her eyes on Lone Wolf. "Every time theres a storm, someone runnin' up here yellin' that the levee gonna break. It ain't broke before, and it ain't gonna break now."

He set the binoculars down. "Looks like the water is rising. If we leave—"

"Fine! But I'm tellin' you, all this is for nothin'. Last time the levee broke, there was a snake givin' Eve a piece of fruit." She wiped her hands on the front of her black dress. "Pee Wee, get me that book and I'll wrap it up for ya nice and tight

"Wolf, can you get my horse?" Teddy took the book from Pee Wee. "We gonna have to hurry and ride back."

"But, Teddy, I don't wanna go. I don't wanna leave the Parish." Pee Wee pushed herself back, deeper into the couch.

"Ya gotta go! There's a whole big world out there, waitin' for a smart girl like you. You learn fast and takes to people quick, and now you got spells and such. You are gonna be such a dangerous young lady that no one will cross your path. Then you come back here and we do rootwork together. I teach you a thing or two not in the book."

Teddy turned and disappeared in the back. "Getcha boots and let's go!"

Pee Wee crossed her arms, defiant. She walked over to the porch and looked out for the water. She heard only the heavy rain and the chickens in the coop fighting for space, but she couldn't see anything—it was too dark—until a crack of lightning illuminated the water. From the flash, she saw that the water was dangerously high and very dark. Suddenly, Pee Wee felt trapped. She imagined the water lapping at Teddy's front door and the ladder downstairs in the dark. The rain was a relentless crashing

"Scat!" Lone Wolf yelled at something and ran up ladder. He stopped near Pee Wee. His hair and clothes were drenched. "We can't leave. The whole path is flooded out."

Pee Wee ran over to the couch and put her boots on. This was not the right time to be defiant. She needed to leave. She wanted to see what Teddy had to say before she gave up hope.

When Teddy walked into the room, also soaked to the bone, Pee Wee knew they weren't going anywhere tonight.

"I gotta getcha home to your ma. She goin' to kill me, not to mention, my brother probably come back and haunt me or somethin'." For the first time, Teddy seemed worried.

"Maybe we can find somethin' in the book to keep him away," Pee Wee said.

Teddy looked at Pee Wee. For a moment, it seemed as though she looked through Pee Wee. All the tension on her face melted away to a warm smile. She walked over and looked out at the waters. She turned and looked at Pee Wee.

"Did ya eat?" Teddy asked.

"Yeah, but not much. You got some biscuits?"

"And fresh honey. I can heat up some biscuits and honey, and then you go to bed and wait out the rain. We gotta get up early and ride over." Teddy led Pee Wee inside the house.

Music was playing, and Pee Wee glanced around, eyes wide, until she saw the phonograph on a table.

"You never heard music before?" Teddy asked.

"Only when I go to town is where I hear this kinda music. I don't even get to go inside; I just hear it in the street."

Lone Wolf held his hand out to her. "Have you even danced with an Indian Miss Pee Wee?"

"Wolf, don't get that child started." Teddy rushed past them toward the kitchen. "We gotta get her to bed so we can leave early."

"Well, Teddy, you were having the party. I'm just making do. No reason for us to sit around and be sad. Pee Wee is gonna go away a kid and come back and see us again. She needs to learn to dance at some point in time." He adjusted his wet hair, which was pulled into a ponytail at the nape of his neck, leaving a trail of dampness running down his back. He twirled and Pee Wee and Teddy saw the wetness of his shirt.

Pee Wee jumped up and down, smiling. "One dance?" she asked Teddy.

"One dance." Teddy nodded her head. "Then to bed with you."

Pee Wee left the box on the couch. She did a little shimmy over to Lone Wolf and took his hand. "Okay, I heard my sister say this to her boyfriend once."

"What'd she say?" Lone Wolf asked.

"She said, 'Learn me some dancin', Big Daddy.'"

Lone Wolf and Teddy stifled a laugh. "She did, now?"

"Show her how to cut a rug!" Teddy yelled as she walked out of the kitchen, holding a plate with warm biscuits.

Pee Wee's bare feet squeaked across the wooden floor as she ran over to Lone Wolf. He motioned for her to stand on his feet. Then, he wrapped an arm around her waist and twirled her around the room to the "Basin Street Blues."

"You sure got some big ol' hands, Mister Wolf." Pee Wee giggled.

The rain continued all night. Even when they finished dancing, and Pee Wee was wrapped up in a blanket on

Teddy's bed, reading the book gifted to her, she heard the rain hitting the roof. She didn't like touching the book, but she loved reading the spells. Besides, she couldn't sleep. She wanted to show Ann what Teddy had made for them, but Ann was sleeping on the couch now anyway. Pee Wee suddenly felt all alone. No one would be able to share her joy but Teddy and Lone Wolf.

She grabbed a folded towel and laid it across her lap so she wouldn't have to keep touching the skin of the cover. She laid the book on top of it and began whispering the spells and mixes aloud as she read them in the lamplight. "Wow, devil's grass and snake head ground up as a powder will blind someone when sprinkled in the ban of a hat. And dust from an anthill will make someone go crazy when you put it in they food."

"Don't mean you need to do it." Teddy murmured. She lay with her back to Pee Wee on the other side of the bed.

"I'm not. It's just...it's a lot." Pee Wee sighed. "How you even keep this straight in your head?"

"When all you do is rootwork, you find a way," Teddy mumbled. Soon, she was snoring.

Pee Wee read until the sunlight crept over the horizon and shone into the room. Her head nodded, but she kept trying to read, holding the book on her lap.

When she felt someone trying to take the book away, she woke up.

"Let me wrap this up," Teddy said, patting Pee Wee on the head. She wore a dark-colored rain slicker. "We are gonna try to go."

"Is it still rainin'?"

"Never stopped." Lone Wolf sat at the table, sipping from a cup and eating a biscuit.

"You think we gonna be okay?" Pee Wee asked.

"Hard to say. Nobody's out. We should assume the levee is broke though." She pulled a slicker out for Pee Wee and tossed it to her.

"Is this for me to wear...or?"

"Protect the book," Teddy told her, putting it back in its box. "It's a one-of-a-kind. When I'm dead and gone, ain't no more. You don't understand how important that book is."

Pee Wee went to the bathroom and got dressed. She slid the slicker over her.

When she came back out, Teddy said, "Lift it up," and pointed to the rain slicker.

Pee Wee held the slicker up, and Teddy fastened the book-box to Pee Wee's chest with a belt.

Pee Wee adjusted it and grunted. She pulled the slicker over the book and snapped the top. "All covered."

Teddy sighed. "All right. Let's go."

MA'S BLUES

Ma shook the rafters, storming through the house that morning, calling for Pee Wee. Ann sat up and kicked Bump off the edge of her mattress. It was hard to tell what time it was because it remained dark and rainy outside the cabin.

"Lord have mercy, if'n you don't stop screamin' in this house!" Skeet sat up on her mattress and fixed the scarf on her head. "Bump, find my cane and make some coffee, boy. This woman 'bout to kill me with all her damned yellin'!"

"Yes'm." he said.

"Where is your sister!" Ma yelled at Ann.

Ann looked at Bump. "Pee Wee say somethin' to you?"

"She say she was gonna look at the bridge last night." He rubbed his eyes. "I thought she come back."

"Sure she ain't upstairs?" Ann asked.

"She ain't here, Patricia Ann." Ma sat in a chair by the door and looked out the window. "We gotta go. The man gonna be here soon."

"Don't look like it stopped rainin'," Bump said.

"Shut up, Bump." Ann snapped. "Ma, don't worry. Pee Wee probably went to see Teddy or somethin'. Ain't nowhere else she could go."

"Just get your stuff together. Take Pee Wee's stuff…"

"I'll watch Pee Wee's stuff," Skeet said. "She trying to come back; I just know it. She don't wanna be left here by herself."

"Pee Wee stubborn like her pa. Hard head, hard behind." Ma pulled out one of Pa's handkerchiefs and wiped her nose.

"I worry for her so much."

"Ma, can I ask you somethin'?" Ann rested her hand on Ma's shoulder. "Last time I saw Betty, I wasn't too nice to her. I'm just wonderin'..."

"Don't talk like that. She'll show up at the finishin' school, I feel it. She got nowhere else to go. I feel it that we goin' to see her again. Don't worry. Betty got sense in her head. She won't do nothin' stupid."

"I told her she was one of the sheriff's babies," Ann mumbled.

Ma looked up at Ann, her eyes red from crying, "Why would you...never mind. She know you didn't mean nothin."

A sharp rap at the door hushed the room, and a tall black man pushed the door open. "I came a bit early. We need to get goin'. I don't like bein' this close to the water with the rain comin' down. I've got a few boys with me to load your stuff."

Ma stood. "Thanks, Pete. I appreciate you comin' early. We just waitin' for my youngest to get back."

Ann busied herself with moving things to the door for the young boys to put in the wagon.

"Mrs. Conway, I don't think much of nothin' is comin' down any path with that storm. I'm hearin' the rivers is floodin'. I'd like to leave as soon as we get packed."

"But...Lord, not two of my girls." Ma groaned.

"Leave some notes and stuff," Skeet said. "I'll get that girl to you! Don't you worry, ol' Skeet will take care of her." She shuffled over to Ma. "Now hush your cryin'. You ain't done nothin' wrong but raised some smart girls. Pee Wee ain't stupid. She comin' back."

Ma collapsed into the chair while the boys moved the stuff to the wagon.

"Stay here. Wait for her," Ma whispered. "My lil Hattie Mae."

"She goin' to be fine. 'Sides, y'all can't get far in this weather. I'll send Bump out to look for ya in the morn. See if you can send one of them street kids back here with news of where y'all at, okay?"

Bump ran into the living room. "I found Pee Wee!"

They all turned. "Where she at?" Ma asked.

"She down the road! They can't get cross cuz the path is all flooded. The levee broke last night, and the way to Teddy's is fillin' up fast. She with Teddy and Lone Wolf." Bump bounced on the balls of his feet. "Come on!!"

Ma showed Skeet what needed to go into the wagon while she put on her rain boots. She grabbed a raincoat and umbrella before she raced out the door. "Take me to her, Bump."

"Let's go!" Ann said, following right behind them.

Bump led the way, running all the way up the path until they saw the trio barely visible through the rain: they looked like not much more than shadows sitting together on horseback on part of the higher ground of the path. Between them, the water flowed fast, almost making white peaks. The rain pounded against everything around them, creating a sound-deafening tunnel.

Pee Wee and Teddy sat on the black horse, next to Lone Wolf on a brown-and-white-spotted horse.

A branch fell into the water, spooking the horses. The animals backed away from the steady moving water, tossing their heads nervously, until Lone Wolf dismounted and tied his to a tree.

When Ma and Ann began hollering, he moved closer to the water to hear them, and Teddy and Pee Wee's horse followed him.

"What?" he yelled at Ma.

Ma, Ann, and Bump moved close to the edge of the water too.

"Let's meet in town or somethin'!" Teddy yelled.

"There's no way to cross," Ma hollered back.

"We can get across!"

Ma shook her head. "No! You stay with Pee Wee, Teddy! You take care of my Pee Wee! We comin' back for you, girl! We can find a way to come back! Just not today! Too much water!"

"I'm sorry, Ma!" Pee Wee yelled. "I'm so sorry. I ain't mean to be a problem! Ma, I can try to swim!"

"No! You stay and find your sister, you hear me! You find her, and we gonna come back for y'all! Do you understand? Got dammit, Hattie Mae!" Ma's voice shook with frustration and anger.

Pee Wee couldn't tell if Ma was angry, and she wondered if Ma could tell that Pee Wee's face was drenched with tears. "I'm sorry," she yelled again. "I love you, Ma!"

"Land's not steady," Lone Wolf shouted. "We gotta get back. The land's gonna give."

They made clicking sounds to their horses and backed away from the water.

Ann stood at the edge of the rushing water. "I'm sorry, Pee Wee! I'm sorry and I love you! Can you hear me, you's a damned fool! I'm coming back for you, ya hear me? Do you hear me, Pee Wee!"

A huge chunk of land collapsed in front of Ma and began sliding away into the water. Bump and Ann pulled Ma back. More water rushed between them.

Ann stretched her hand out for her sister.

"I love you! I'm comin' back, I promise! I don't mean to be no trouble! I wanna go with you." Pee Wee struggled on the horse behind Teddy.

"Sit down on this horse! Don't you dare get off!" Teddy grabbed the belt beneath Pee Wee's slicker.

"But...but...my sister..." Pee Wee cried.

"It's too late now," Lone Wolf said. He untied his horse and started leading it away. There came another sound of tree branches cracking. "Ladies, we've gotta go! It's gonna give!"

The tree toppled and crashed into the floodwaters below, splashing them all with water.

The tree was quickly submerged before other cracks sounded in trees along the waterline.

Ann stretched her hand out in the direction of her sister across the water. She imagined that she was touching Pee Wee one last time. She felt bad for all the things she'd said and done.

Pee Wee held her arm out and imagined reaching over to Ann. "I'm sorry I'm stupid. I can't believe I done somethin' so stupid. Now I lost both my sisters."

"Don't talk like that!" Teddy said. "You see them again soon, if we get back to higher ground. I promise." She yanked the reins, and the horse turned and scampered up the muddy hill.

One of the boys who had been with Pete came running down the trail toward them. "He say we gotta go now," he told Ma.

Ma looked at Pee Wee and raised her hand to wave. She blew her a kiss. "Stay strong. I'll be back. Teddy, take care of my baby."

Ann pulled Ma back as the mud near the water's edge loosened more.

Ma looked up at the sky and cried out, "God! You take care of them! You owe me, Lord. Not one Sunday I missed church. I always tithe. You watch over them, Lord!"

Then they turned and ran back to the house as the rain slammed harder into them.

A NEW BEGINNING

Three weeks later, Pee Wee was finally able to make it back to the cabin. All the roads had been washed away. All the secret little cutaways they'd taken to get around were gone. The forest was one huge mud-swamp. Trudging through the mud toward her house, she saw Skeet sweeping the porch and felt a warmth she'd been missing since she last saw her Ma waving to her over the water.

"Skeet!" Pee Wee ran and hugged Skeet. "Hope you takin' good care of my house."

"Aw girl! I knew you was comin' back. Come on in."

Skeet opened the door, and Pee Wee stepped inside the half empty house. On the floor, there were outlines where furniture had once sat. Now, there was the bed in Ma and Pa's room, and a table in the kitchen. Skeet had a small mattress placed on the floor for Bump to sleep on.

When Bump heard Pee Wee, he jumped up from reading a book that Ann left for him. "You back!"

Pee Wee hugged him. "Yeah, I said I was comin'."

"It's been almost a month." Skeet worked her way to the chair at the kitchen table. "Ann took your stuff upstairs, and that's where it's been. I sleep down here. My lil ol' shack was washed away."

Pee Wee hugged Skeet. "Skeet, you can stay here as long as you need. I'm gonna keep workin' with Teddy 'til I make enough money to go to my ma. Then, I'm gonna take care a her too. And Ann. And Betty. We all gonna be together, and we gonna come back to the parish."

"Well, I wasn't leavin', child. I'm too old, too black, and too tired to keep movin' around like y'all think I can." She laughed. "'Sides, apple don't fall far from the tree. Rootwork run in your blood, strong. And your sister left this for ya."

Skeet reached into a pocket on the front of her apron and gave Pee Wee a letter from Ann.

"We ain't read it," Bump said. "Promise."

Pee Wee read the letter:

Sis,

I could spend all this letter telling you how mad I am at you for leaving me and running away to Aunt Teddy's. But I'm not mad. I wish I would have left too. I know, in your heart, you didn't want to leave the parish. It feel like something takes a hold of you and roots you to the ground here. You try to leave, but it pull you back, and you never get too far.

I understand because I feel like that too. And that's why I'm telling you this. I'm coming back. You don't worry about Ma. I'll take care of her. You practice and do that rootwork with Teddy. You be the best conjure woman in this parish when I come back, you understand?! I want to see you being independent and your own person, not having to depend on nobody or nothing. And when I come back, we'll get Betty, and we will celebrate being together.

You and her are all I got left in this world. I really miss you lots. It's hard not hearing you snore in the bed, or sleeping with Betty under her mosquito nets, but I have my memories.

I also saved enough and got this made for you. I found it in Pa's wallet, so I figure I get one for me, one for you, and one for Betty. If you see her, you give it to her.

Ma is taking this hard, thinking she did something wrong. But I know the truth. You know the truth. Ma not ready for the truth. I will help her understand, and maybe, in time, she come back to the parish too.

Skeet got the keys to the place. We told her she could stay there 'til you come back. Most the village gone anyway, so don't make no sense for her to go looking somewhere else to live when she got a good house right there.

I love you, Hattie Mae. You tell Betty that I love her too. And when I see you again, it's gonna be a day we ain't never gonna forget.

Your sister and friend,
Patricia Ann Conway

"What it say?" Bump asked.

"It say that I need to thump you in the head, that's what it say." Pee Wee folded the letter and put it in her pocket. She felt something fall, and squatted to pick it up. It was two pictures of the same thing: Pee Wee and her sisters, all standing outside the house with Ma and Pa, smiling. She remembered Ann saved money and Betty helped with what Ann couldn't save. It was a Christmas present from all of them to Ma and Pa. Now, Pee Wee had a copy of the picture made for her and Betty. If she ever saw Betty in town, she'd give it to her.

"Skeet, I'm gonna take some stuff and stay with Teddy. I promise I'll take care of you and Bump though. I'll bring ya food and money and whatever you need, okay? Bump, you come with me to Teddy's, so you can learn the new way to get there. Take a little longer, but…" Pee Wee shrugged her shoulders. "I can't change the land or nothin.'"

When they reached Teddy's place, Pee Wee hugged Bump goodbye before he set off back to the house. She told him that he could come get her whenever he needed something.

"I'll be back next week, okay?" she said. "Take care of Skeet and my house."

"Sure." Bump nodded.

Pee Wee spent the day around her house, cleaning. She gathered a few things to make Teddy's place feel more like a home. She packed a sack and threw it over her shoulder when she headed back to Teddy's down a newer and higher path to Teddy's place.

Later in the afternoon, she climbed the ladder to Teddy's.. She pulled a familiar hand-decorated box from her sack that Betty used to store her sewing stuff in. It was a way to tie all the sisters together.

She took the book from the box, wrapped it in a blood-red silk cloth, then gently placed it back inside and closed the lid.

"You ready?" Teddy stood behind her, with her hands behind her back.

Pee Wee nodded. "Ready."

"Let's get you set and get started." Teddy pulled a black head wrap from behind her back. She tied it on Pee Wee's head and showed her in the mirror how she looked.

Pee Wee turned her face from side to side and smiled at herself. In her eyes, she looked older and wiser than the beginning of the summer.

Teddy smiled in the mirror behind her before putting her hand on Pee Wee's shoulder, "Let's get to doin' some rootwork."

ACKNOWLEDGMENTS

I promised Marcus Garvey Powell in high school that he would get this first line. Here's to you Marcus.

Sadie Hartmann ("Mother Horror") and Rob Carroll, thanks for giving me a place to share my story. Thanks for reaching out and believing in me. And Sadie, I can't ever thank you enough for everything you've done and continue to do. Even though you are "Mother Horror," you are one of the good ones that walk on this Earth, and I am honored to be in your presence and on your imprint!!

I also want to thank my friends for encouraging me and reaching out: Jennifer Pocock for her help with all the research I needed. I need to thank my sister, Teri Ellen Cross Davis, for inspiration and being an awesome sister. Thanks Mom and Dad (Burnetta and Raymond) for listening to different iterations of parts of this book. And my mother for sharing her memories with me. Thanks to my grandmas, Katie Mae York and Vergie "Tootsie" Cross, for the stories about the South. My great aunts, Lola Mae Blackmon, and Betty Jean Berry, for teaching me about gardening and sharing stories that I wasn't supposed to share with their older sister, Katie Mae. Thanks to Eddie Lovelace, Jack Cross III, Patricia "Ann" York, Debbye Cross, Marshall York Jr., Uncle Bear, and Brenda Lee York.

Big thanks to the Capitol Hill Writers Group and my peers AhXul and Lyl and even Ariel. (And recently Anastasia and Emily.) Thanks to Howard, Mac, Mickey, Mary L., Brandon Johnson, and Brandon M for coming to a few of my joint readings. Thanks Mig Dooley for always having a camera and a smile when I call. TaChalla F., Ana Elisa (for answering every neurotic phone call and text message), Jess Stork, Paul Richardson, John Lyon, and Shay for being voluntary readers as well. I appreciate your time and feedback. I also want to thank my brother-in-law, Hayes, for his sprinkling of a word or two here and there to help me improve. Toni, my sister, for not having the courage to jump into the fear with me but sharing some of the stories from Lola.

Huge thanks to Marissa van Uden for some great editing and making magic and wonder happen for this book.

Kate Jonez, Sean Patrick Traver, Lisa Morton, thanks for giving me all these opportunities (and responding to all my emails when I had a million questions and to whom I owe exactly one Arby's meal).

Also, Kate Maruyama, Raw Dog Screaming Press, Jason Henderson and Brian McAuley (we've just started this journey together, let's keep going!) and Lisa Pegram for some last-minute help.

I also want to shout out the Horror Writers Association for their support.

Here's to the future readers, my kids, niece, and nephews, Raena, Rafael, Sofía, Zoë, Malik and August. The future is in your hands.

José-muchas gracias para todo

Thank you, reader, for purchasing this book.

Sincerely,

Tracy Cross

ABOUT THE AUTHOR

Tracy Cross is a horror writer based in Washington, D.C. She is an active member of the Horror Writer's Association and was a recipient of the association's "Scholarship From Hell" in 2022. *Rootwork* is her first published novel. For more information about Tracy, or to catch up on her latest exploits, visit her website at tracycrossonline.com.

Also Available from Dark Hart Books

All These Subtle Deceits by C. S. Humble
ISBN 978-1-958598-04-7

All the Prospect Around Us by C. S. Humble
ISBN 978-1-958598-05-4

Mosaic by Catherine McCarthy
ISBN 978-1-958598-06-1

Available from Dark Matter INK

Human Monsters: A Horror Anthology
edited by Sadie Hartmann and Ashley Saywers
ISBN 978-1-958598-00-9

Linghun by Ai Jiang
ISBN 978-1-958598-02-3

Monstrous Futures: A Sci-fi Horror Anthology
edited by Alex Woodroe
ISBN 978-1-958598-07-8

Haunted Reels: Stories From the Minds of Professional Filmmakers curated by David Lawson
ISBN 978-1-958598-13-9

Frost Bite by Angela Sylvaine
ISBN 978-1-958598-03-0

Monster Lairs: A Dark Fantasy Horror Anthology
edited by Anna Madden
ISBN 978-1-958598-08-5

The Bleed by Stephen S. Schreffler
ISBN 978-1-958598-11-5

The Bones Beneath Paris by Kelsea Yu
ISBN 978-1-958598-12-2

CPSIA information can be obtained
at www.ICGtesting.com
Printed in the USA
LVHW100043010323
740595LV00003B/460

9 781958 598016